Contents

CW01080839

CHAPTER ONE : THE BEGINNING

CHAPTER TWO : A NEW FRIEND

CHAPTER THREE: DETENTION, AND A DEADLY DISRUPTION

CHAPTER FOUR: A LARGE WIN AND DANCE PREPARATION

CHAPTER FIVE : THREE IMPORTANT EVENTS

CHAPTER SIX : JANNETE, APRIL, MAE, AND JUNE'S BIG LIE

CHAPTER SEVEN : ROGERERARE

CHAPTER EIGHT: LOUIS LETTERS, AND MIDNIGHT MURDERING

CHAPTER NINE : NIGHTMARE AT WINGED BEAUTIES

CHAPTER TEN: BREAK IN

CHAPTER ELEVEN: COTTAGE GRIEF

CHAPTER TWELVE: ROASI STREET

CHAPTER THIRTEEN: BLOODHILL MANOR

CHAPTER FOURTEEN: NO CONTACT

CHAPTER FIFTEEN: THE THREE Rs

CHAPTER SIXTEEN: PENNSYLVANIA

CHAPTER SEVENTEEN: THE ONE GOODBYE THAT RIPS YOUR HEART FOREVER

CHAPTER EIGHTEEN: THE END OF ONE, THE BEGINNING, OF ANOTHER

Wings

A New Life

CHAPTER ONE : THE BEGINNING

Luna Copper lives at 74 Moonlight Avenue. She lives with her Granny and her Grandpa because her parents had perished in an unknown incident. She had never really known them but had seen signs that they were still alive, somewhere deep and psychological yet still unidentified. She had only gotten to spend the first year and a half of her life with them. Living with her grandparents wasn't the best situation even though she loved and cared about them dearly and would be outstandingly depressed if anything would have happened to either of them. Her and her grandparents were accompanied by Luna's cousin Alex, whose parents were not dead but were simply on their honeymoon on the opposite side of the country. Alex was a rather skinny teenager who had only just turned 14.

Luna's grandparents were very fond of Alex but not so much Luna. She shared a room with Alex but was given nowhere near as exciting materials as her cousin was. Mr and Mrs Silverhood had decided to split the girl's room in half, deliberately making Luna's side of the room increasingly smaller. Whilst they decorated Alex's side of the room Luna was told to do the same to her part of the room with nothing but a mattress and a few barrels of paint that had clearly been bought from the two dollar shop across the street. In the space of half an hour she had finished and was strictly instructed to go and mow the lawn, so that's exactly what she did.

After just finishing the right side of the lawn she heard light footsteps and then a rather urgent knock on the front door. Luna just shrugged her shoulders and began the left side of the lawn, until she heard it again; only much firmer this time, as if someone really wanted in. She heard the slamming of her bedroom door and the grunt of her Grandpa through the open window. She heard the knock again and then a male, squeaky voice beamed through the letterbox.

"Oi! Le' me in! A wud lik' tae speak wi' Luna Coppr' pleas'! An' if you dinae le' me in noo then a hav' every right tae blas' the door off wi' ma bare hands. So le' me in!" The moment she heard the words Luna and Copper come through the letterbox she ran inside excitedly with a ball of grass in her hand yelling "It's for me! It's for MEEE!"

"Oi!" yelled Mr Silverhood and he gripped Luna firmly by the shoulders and stuck his hand over her mouth to stop her screaming. "Get the door Molly." He said to Mrs Silverhood, and she opened the door before you could say terrified. A small midget man waddled into the hall with a noticeboard.

"I've cam' froom the Winged Bein' Abuse Prevention Offic' and wud lik' it if you removed yur hands froom that wee girls mooth pleas." said the small man. Mr Silverhood removed his hand from Luna's mouth. "The names Barney Bubwul." the man said.

Barney stretched out his hand to shake Mr Silverhood's but Mr Silverhood snatched his hand away as if he had just held burning metal. Barney turned away on his tiny heel and said "Well" in a way that made it seem like he was somehow hurt by Luna's Grandfathers behaviour. He pointed at Luna in utter admiration and said. "You mus' bae Luna. I'v' heard a lo' aboot ya, yur parents were so excited wen' Vicky go' pregnant wi' you." Lunas eyes widened.

"Sir? Sorry but did you just say my... My er parents?" Luna was hoping and crossing her fingers behind her back that this was just a bad dream.

Sadly, Barney replied, "Yea' real shame they crashed intae a military plane. A cot you a metr' froom the floar."

Luna now had tears in her eyes, ignoring the roar of anger upon Mr Silverhood's face.

Luna said. "How did they crash? Were they pilots? I always thought they were both... Huh?"

Barney said. "No Luna. No no no. They cood flae themselves Luna."

"WHAT!" roared Luna. The next thing she knew she was in a huge white room with hospital beds everywhere.

There were lots of injured children on the beds and she noticed that she was one of them, she had a broken arm! She was wearing something completely different though. A blue tartan skirt, a black cardigan and a blue top. A small blonde headed little boy opposite Luna said in a small voice, "Mrs Penny." and an average woman came over to Luna.

The woman said. "Oh, you're up, good. You fainted at the Silverhood house darling, so Barney thought you ought to come here. To the hospital wing of Winged Beauties Boarding School for Children with the Gift. Now drink this. It should get you through your first couple of classes but if not then just tell your professor okay? I'm Mrs Penny by the way, Head of the Hospital." She said it rather proudly.

She handed Luna a miniature plastic cup of what looked like a small portion of zombie vomit. Luna stared at it. "Swallow it then!" Mrs Penny roared before choking it down Lunas throat and walking her to the door. Before either of them could say any more the door in front of them opened and a tall man with giant white wings and a white moustache entered. He had clearly gotten a fright that Luna was standing there but kept a rather calm facial expression. His voice was deep but kind. He said, "Hello Luna, Hello Margaret. I believe I need to have a little chat with Luna in private."

Mrs Penny went to go and look at the blonde boy. The tall man motioned Luna to her hospital bed and she laid on it. The man closed the leather red curtains and sat down next to Luna's bed. "Hello. I'm Rogererare and I am the headmaster of the school. You've probably not got a clue what this place is or what you're doing here. It is a school for gifted children like you who have the power to fly. There are five classes you will attend, exactly five. If you miss one of the then your professor has every right to give you detention, which will take place in my office. The classes are: Wingcare and Maintenance class with Lady Gatherhow, Wing Picking class with Professor Olcear, Flying class with Madam Spannel, Wing Painting class with Sir Davie, and Winghinging class with Professor Fire." Luna gave him a confused look before he continued talking.

"Winghinging is a sport we have here. It works by using your wings to fly and catch a ball for your team. There are two Winghinging teams, Ravens and Eagles. There are three types of balls: Two red ones named the Cags which are worth nothing, a brown ball named the Wogger, and a blue ball called the Coka. In each team there are four players: the Hitters which there are two of, they try to score goals with the Wogger for ten points; one Goaler, they guard the hoops from the opposite team; and the Finder who tries to get the Coka. The Coka is worth five hundred points! Its mega fast and it can teleport. The balls named Cags are flying about trying to knock people down. If you touch the floor then you are out. Get it?"

Luna nodded as if hypnotised. Rogererare said, "Oh and Luna, here's your Winglet. It's a pet and a mail carrier." He pulled out a cage with what looked like a mini pair of wings. It had adorable little eyes. It was blue and was flapping around the cage.

"Rogererare", said Luna. "Can we talk about my parents more tomorrow?" Rogererare just winked, opened the curtains and left.

As Luna laid there, still and confused, it suddenly hit her that she could FLY! She sat up immediately grasping her spine, Picked up her Winglet cage and sprinted for the door. Until she was stopped. "What do you think you're doing out of bed little lady." It was Mrs Penny.

"Ugh... Just umm... Getting more medicine." Said Luna, whilst pointing to a strange shaped container of the zombie vomit medicine.

"Oh do you think you need more darling?" Said Mrs Penny in a kind way. "Why didn't you say so?" she said as she got another plastic cup. She filled it up and handed it to Luna. Without even thinking, Luna just shoved it in her mouth. It was only once she had tasted it that she spat it out, but in the wrong place.

"LUNA!" yelled Mrs Penny, whilst watching the medicine pour down her white plaited hospital uniform.

Luna's jaw dropped. She ran down the corridor and found herself in a female toilet. She shut herself in a cubicle until a girl's voice sounded, "Who's there?"

"I'm Luna, Luna Copper." Said Luna.

The voice said, "Oh."

"What's your name?" asked Luna.

"Coco" said the voice.

"Hello Coco, would it be possible to meet you in person?" Said Luna.

"Ok" Said Coco.

They both simultaneously opened their doors. They both were extremely surprised at the sight of each other. Luna, who was a very very very dark haired little girl, saw a girl, who not only looked awfully a lot like Alex, but seemed the same age as Luna. Her hair was a violent shade of ginger and she was holding something that looked like a small cat that had wings.

Coco looked at the Winglet cage Luna had forgotten she was holding and said "Wow! Is that a Winglet?"

Luna said "Er... Yeah?" Coco admired it.

"I'm stuck with this." She said whilst looking at her small cat sadly. "She was my brother Charles's Cwinger but he moved to Africa to raise his child."

Luna said "Cool."

"What's your Winglets name?" Said Coco.

Luna replied, "Wait... Your supposed to name it? Er... I'll name it Baw...lo...siph...er."

Coco giggled and said, "Bawlosipher?"

"Y...Ye...Yeah" Said Luna. "I mean, what did you have in mind?"

Coco looked at the creature with her head tilted sideways. "Well, it's er...Gleeful, a little weak and blue so... What about Glee?"

Luna nodded and said "OK." They both giggled whilst skipping down the corridor. As they walked past a room, that they assumed was a library, an older girl and two other girls who were clearly in their last years of school stepped out.

The smaller girl said, "Hi, I'm Jasmine. This is Katie and Jennifer. I see you're hanging around with a Wheezleberry. If you want to make friends you'll have to hang out with the popular crowd. That's us." She put her hand out to shake Luna's, with the other she clicked her fingers. Katie and Jennifer walked over and took Coco's Cwinger! They walked away and Jennifer kicked Coco in the shins so hard that she fell over.

Whilst Luna helped her up Coco yelled. "Oh No! My Cwinger! She tried to run down the corridor after them but only managed to limp. "Brownie!"

Luna couldn't help but snort at the name. "Brownie? It's a white cat Coco." Coco just smirked at her. She tried to run again but Luna caught her before she tripped over a radiator.

"Come on Coco... We need to get you to the hospital wing." Said Luna breathily. As they supported each other Jasmine, Katie and Jennifer came over clutching their chest sarcastically.

"Oh. Has little Copper and little Wheezleberry got booboos. Aaaawww. How pathetic. HA." Spat Jasmine.

Coco said, "Shut up Jasmine." Jasmine, Katie and Jennifer tutted, flicked their hair and walked away. Coco mimicked them comically and Luna sniggered. By the time they had reached the hospital there was a large crowd of students gathered around the blonde boy's bed. Coco tried to look over but Luna steered her to her own previous bed. She put Glee's cage down and the two girls laid down. After a long while Mrs Penny came over. She was muttering something under her breath in some kind of code. As Luna listened all of the other sounds in the wing aired out and it was just Mrs Penny's muttering.

"What was she saying?" Thought Luna. But then it went away and all of the other sounds came back.

Unremarkably, Mrs Penny said, "Here. Drink this then you'd better be off." She handed them each a cup of bright green liquid. They both tasted it and it tasted of mashed potatoes. Mrs Penny shooed them away and they went over to the boy's bed. He laid there, motionless. He had purple marks all over his face and his eyes were staring at the roof blankly. There was poison ivy all over his bed. Luna noticed that Jasmine was holding Brownie by her tail over the poison ivy!

Luna yelled. "Coco look! It's Brownie!" Coco jumped, grabbed Brownie but got caught around the wrist by the poison ivy.

"LUNA! She screamed as she threw the cat into Luna's arms. Luna ran and placed Brownie tentatively into Glee's cage. She went back to Coco, everyone had left and Mrs Penny was doing surgery on a patient down the corridor miles away. Coco had gone blue and looked as though she was trying to catch an invisible fly.

"No no NO!" yelled Luna, panicking. She went to the door to see if anyone out there could help, but no luck. By the time she had gotten back to Coco, the poison ivy had spread all over her body and was holding her high in the air. It all of a sudden threw her to the floor. The bang made Luna fall to the floor in shock. CLICK. She had landed on her broken arm. Coco sat up, coughing and spluttering. Miraculously, Coco seemed okay, except she was swearing loudly about how Jasmine was a (word I cannot repeat), and how she was going to kill her. Luna could barely hear her, her arm was too painful. She closed her eyes tightly and when she opened them she was on a trolley with the lower part of her left arm hanging off! She was bleeding madly and she was dripping all over the floor.

"Are you okay?" Screamed Coco as she ran up to the trolley. "Mrs Penny is going to give you a cast and then she told me to take you back to the dormitories. Here's Glee." She tried to hand Glee's cage to Luna before remembering that she probably couldn't hold it at that point of time. She placed Glee at the bottom of the trolley.

"Your dormitory isn't ready yet so you're sleeping with me tonight. I took Brownie back to my dorm so she is safe by the way." Coco said. Luna nodded tiredly.

Mrs Penny arrived quickly with a cast ready. She adjusted it onto Luna's wounded arm and said, "Oh darling, how does that feel?" Luna just nodded again. Coco helped her to the door of her dormitory. It was poorly decorated. All it had in it was a bed and a chair made out of dark wood, she had a white curtain around her double bed. To Luna however it was magical, compared to her room back at the Silverhood house.

"Wow!" Said Luna in admiration.

"What?" Said Coco. "It's horrible. My family only just has enough money to pay the bills for our house. Mum works at a cheese making place and Dad works for the Winged Being Abuse Prevention Office as a trainer. He actually used to play Hitter in the American Ravens team, but that was years ago. He was twenty-one back then. That place actually belongs to my biggest brother Jackson. I have five of them, brothers that is. I only have two sisters. The oldest is Jackson, he's twenty-seven. Then its Charles, he's nineteen. Then its Rachel, she's eighteen. Next is Ryan, he's sixteen. Then its

Finn, he's fourteen. Then its Bill, he's fourteen too. They're twins. Then it's me, I'm twelve. Then its Amber, she's six." Luna found it rather difficult to keep track of all of that information but one thing she couldn't forget was, 'And Dad works for the Winged Being Abuse Prevention Office.'

She said, "Wait, hold on. Did you say your Dad works for the Winged Being Abuse Prevention Office?"

"Yeah" Replied Coco.

Luna said "Did he know Barney Bubwul?"

"Oh yes, yes he did but he wishes he hadn't. Horrible man he is, a killer say some, a ghost say others. I think he's the one who killed Andrew Hooding. He's lived since 1701. He made something that makes him never die but no one knows what. He can control ivy. I reckon he was controlling the one that attacked me. Apparently he's tried to kill Rogererare, multiple times but he's never succeeded. One time on April the nineteenth 1998 he just woke up and decided to fly a military plane, cloned himself in case something bad happened. He knocked two fliers' wings off! No one has seen any sight of him since but he has left notes, clues and blood spillages everywhere he has stricken." Said Coco.

Luna was shocked but quite upset that Barney had lied.

She said, "A military plane? Two fliers'?" Coco's angry face went kind. She wrapped her arm around Luna.

"What's wrong?" She said whilst watching the tears pour down Luna's face.

Luna said, "Well, C...Coco the...The...Those f...F...Fliers we...were...were my...Er...My parents."

Coco said, "Oh... I...I...I... Am so...Er...So sorry Luna I...I...Didn't know."

Luna shook her head sadly and got into bed, with her back turned to Coco and her heart broken. Coco sighed and sat on her large windowsill. She cried and rested her head on the glass. She saw the snow below move. She saw two bright green eyes now. As a figure rose up above the soft white sheet of snow Coco fainted and Luna stared in astonishment. She saw the familiar face of the small man she had met at her Grandparent's house, who goes by the name of Barney, Barney Bubwul. He began to pick the lock on the window with one sharp and chipped fingernail. As Luna took a step towards her collapsed friend Barney knocked on the window with three loud bangs against the glass. To Luna's astonishment, several strong men, who looked as though they were made of coal, marched from the dark, cold areas of the room. They gripped Luna at every part of her body you could think of, and weren't letting go. Luna tried her hardest to get out of their arms but the men gripped her tighter. It felt like she was a piece of clay. Luna felt herself getting weaker and weaker by the minute. "Hhhhheeeeelllllppppp!" she squealed, but it was too late. Barney slid the window open slowly and stepped inside. Luna noticed he had what looked like an ancient pocket knife. He was laughing hysterically.

"Well, well, well, another Copper I see. Well this will be rather easy. I wish you well for trying to save your friend." Barney said in a hoarse voice.

"I will save her! And you'll be sorry." Luna said, foolishly. The men held her even tighter and she could feel herself getting sleepier and sleepier. She said, tiredly, "What do you want from us, but more importantly what are you going to do to us?"

"Well, to answer your first question, I want your friend's body as I was shrunk as punishment when I was in prison for murder. To answer your second and final question, I'm here to make you an offer." He said unhurriedly.

Luna said "What?"

"Well, I was thinking something like, I get one of your bodies one way or another and you, Luna, are the lucky girl who chooses. I will get your friend's body or yours, you pick." Said Barney.

"I can't pick." Luna said sadly.

"Suit yourself." Said Barney, "I guess I will kill the one who is closer." He took the knife out of his pocket and took a few steps towards an unconscious Coco.

"NO!" Luna yelled, tugging desperately to get out of coal men's arms. "No." She said slowly. "No." She started to cry. "No Coco." She fell to her knees. "My friend, no Coco."

Coco sat up quickly, but before she could say anything the whole room flooded with students who had heard the screams of what sounded like a young girl being murdered.

CHAPTER TWO: A NEW FRIEND

Luna collapsed to her knees, crying. All of the other first-years crouched next to her with sad facial expressions. Suddenly everyone moved to the sides of the room as Rogererare stepped through the door, accompanied by three hospital maids.

He said, "What is going on here?" He looked at the probably-dead Coco. "Who is responsible for this?" He yelled, "Would you please step forward so I know whose parent or guardian to call." Barney stepped forward with a proud smirk displayed across his smug face. Rogererare said, "Barney Nicho Bubwul. Why on *earth* do you think you have any right whatsoever to come into this school and kill a first year little girl."

Barney replied, "I needed another kill Arthur. I've not gotten to do one for many years. Just needed to get one more kill off my chest." He and the coal men all disappeared and the scene was just full of terrified children and a headmaster.

Rather urgently Rogererare said, "Everyone to the dormitories. Luna Copper, stay." A dark-haired hospital maid knelt down by Coco and said to the others, "This girl is still alive, we need to get her to the hospital wing immediately." Once the maids and the other students had left the room

Luna dried her eyes and walked over to Rogererare. "Luna. Have you... By any chance, met Barney before?"

Luna took a deep breath and said. "Yes. Yes I have. He came to my house. But he seemed nice, and he had a Scottish accent. He said he had come from the Winged Being Abuse Prevention Office. He invited me here Rogererare."

Rogererare sighed in relief and said. "Oh, oh phew. Don't you worry about that Luna. He works here. He's one of the clones of the real Barney Bubwul. Except he was made differently. He wouldn't dare hurt a soul, and he has a part time job at the Winged Being Abuse Prevention Office.

Luna nodded and asked politely, "Er... Rogererare. Sorry to change the subject but where will I be sleeping tonight?" Rogererare tried his best to put a faint smile on his face.

"Oh. Well if you take Glee and Brownie and follow me if you'd please. Rogererare handed the pet cage to Luna and she followed him to a door along the hall from the room they were in before. He opened it to reveal a room. An incredible room. It had a rose wood bed with blue sheets and a fluffed white pillow, a rose wood chair along with a blue pillow fitted neatly on top of it, a rose wood shelving unit lined with every book for every class, a rose wood trunk, a rather large blue rug, a smaller rug in front of the bookshelf and a new cage for Glee. Flying around the room was a painted picture of two handsome people. One male and one female. Holding a tiny baby.

Luna's mouth opened. "Is this... Is this my... My dormitory?" She said

"Yes Luna. And those are your parents holding you." Rogererare replied. He pointed to the flying painting. "Really!" Replied Luna in shock. She had almost forgotten about the incident in Coco's dormitory. Except, then she remembered.

"Oh... Rogererare, it's amazing but is it okay if I go and check on Coco?" She said politely. Rogererare nodded and Luna shuffled along to the hospital wing. She wandered along the long rows of injured children until she found Coco on bed 244. She kneeled next to the bed, biting her lip and stroking her friends arm. But the night rose and fell. Along with the next three. Luckily after what felt like forever, Mrs Penny rushed over carrying a cup full of thick white gloop. She tentatively poured it into Coco's mouth and Coco burst upwards into a sitting position.

Mrs Penny sighed in relief and comfortably said. "Phew, Miss Wheezleberry is going to be okay. Just a temporary case of Margatosis." Luna and Coco looked at each other blankly and Mrs Penny looked at them as if they were idiots.

"Margatosis? You don't know what it is?" She said with her jaw wide. The two girls shook their heads. Mrs Penny walked along the corridor with her head in her hands muttering something that sounded awfully like "Youngsters." Luna jumped in excitement. "Oh my god you're okay!" she yelped. She jumped at Coco and wrapped her arms around her.

Whilst trying to detach Luna from her body Coco said, "I'm fine but what happened?" Luna shook her head wildly and said, "You don't even want to know."

Coco smiled comfortably and replied, "Okay, so don't tell me. I really really want to go to the library to figure out what Margatosis is though. Can we go?"

Luna thought for a moment and said, "Okay. We might need to ask someone where it is though. I was laughing too much to really notice it before we met Jasmine." Coco nodded and they both sneaked behind Mrs Penny and ran out of the hospital wing cheerfully. They looked in different rooms and doors, and at one point found themselves not in a library but in another bathroom. They saw the sign on the door noting. MALE RESIDENTS ONLY. "Oops." Coco whispered. They turned around and reached for the doorknob but not before a male voice beamed at them.

"Ahem. What do you two *girls* think you're doing in the *boy's* bathroom? Can't you read? It's clearly stated on the door."

Luna replied, "We, er... we... Were... Umm, well... we were.... Looking... Looking for the... umm... The library." The boy laughed.

"Oh well I can help you with that. Follow me if you'd please." He said. He led the two embarrassed girls down a thin corridor and into a room stacked with books everywhere.

"I'm Louis by the way." The boy said. "You are?"

Luna shook his hand and replied. "I'm Luna, this is my friend Coco."

"Oh well nice to meet you two. Would you like me to help you look for something?" Said Louis kindly.

Coco replied, "Um yes. We are looking for a book to help us find out what Margatosis is, Mrs Penny told me I have a case of it."

"Oh! I've never heard of that but I'll see what I can find." Louis said. They all ran in different directions to start looking. After about an hour Louis yelled. "Hey girls! I don't know if this will help but I have found something!" The three of them rushed to a table surrounded by beanbags. He threw a large, brown book in the middle of the table and said, "Will this help?" The book was titled, **'Un Coding Murmurs.'**

"How is that gonna help?" Coco said impatiently.

Louis said, "Well, Luna said that Mrs Penny was muttering something right?" Luna nodded. "Well. We can figure out what she was muttering with this book. Tell you what. I'll go borrow this and you two meet me in the 'West Hall' okay?" The girls nodded and set off for the 'West Hall.' Once they had sat down Coco said quietly, "I have a secret about Louis." "What!" Luna yelled.

"Ssshhh!" Coco said, but she was giggling. "Well it's the nineteenth of December and on the twenty-sixth there's a Christmas ball. And... Well I kinda... Maybe want to invite him to it." She was biting her lip.

"Coco. You only *met Louis* like an hour and a half ago." Luna sniggered.

"Oh I know but... Oh no! He's coming... Shut it Luna. I mean it." Coco said. Luna nodded and slouched on her chair. Louis hurriedly ran into the hall with three books.

He sat breathlessly beside Luna and panted, "Ok, So, I borrowed a few books; Un Coding Murmurs, Definitions of Dangerous Diseases and Flying Catastrophes."

"Once again Louis, how is Flying Catastrophes going to help us?" Coco angrily whispered.

Louis replied patiently, "Oh *that* one won't help. I just needed it to study for our flying class with Madam Spannel this afternoon."

"Oh no!" Luna yelped, "I forgot about that class today, our first class and I haven't even prepared. I'm going to go and get my books from my dormitory, wait a second." She ran out of the room and returned a few minutes afterwards with a stack of books in her arms. She placed them on the table and stared at Coco, who was reading with a rather worrying expression.

"Er... Guys, I er... Don't know how to er tell you this but, well. I know what Margatosis is." She said.

Luna squealed, "WHAT?"

"Well Luna, it says here, 'anyone under the age of fifteen will experience a severe allergic reaction to any water related liquid. Symptoms include rashes, memory loss, and sometimes an official death.' Coco said calmly.

"The Puddlefly!" Louis said whilst whacking himself on the forehead with his hand.

"Excuse me?" The girls simultaneously said.

Louis replied, "Tonight, in flying class. We're doing an assessment, an assessment on flying over different landscapes, and unfortunately one of them is a lake!" The girls gasped and Coco looked like she had just seen her grandmother in a bikini.

"Ok, we can deal with this, I have a plan. Coco, do what you can, Luna, mark me as absent today and make sure nothing *too* bad happens. I'll try to figure out what Mrs Penny was saying, it might give us some sort of clue." The girls nodded, held each other's hands and went out to the grounds.

As they arrived they realised that Madam Spannel was a tall skinny woman who tied her black silky hair in a tight bun which made her forehead seem as large as Coco's entire head. She seemed to be one of those people who had a constant expression on their face that looked as though they had just eaten a rotten egg and washed it down with lumpy milk.

She yelled, "Class!" She started pacing the grounds, "I am Madam Spannel and I will be giving you your practice wings today. I expect that all of you have read chapters forty-one through two-hundred and twelve of Top Tips and Tricks by Andrew Hooding's father Tom Hooding, am I correct? The entire class nodded whilst Coco and Luna stood there puzzled.

"I've only read chapters forty-one through fifty-six." Coco anxiously said.

"Here are your practice wings!" Madam Spannel yelled. She tossed around eighteen pairs of glossy white wings onto the grass. "You will simply attach them to your bodies like shown in chapter sixty-one and you will complete the course. Am I clear?" Once again the class nodded and put their wings onto their backs.

"How the hell do you do that?" Coco moaned. Madam Spannel marched over like a soldier.

"I see that neither of you have gotten your ripping operation done yet, no? Well perhaps it is worth me doing it at the moment so that you two can take the test." She stepped behind them, put her left hand on Coco's back, put her right one on Luna's, and she shoved her fingernail down through their skin about a centimetre down. Although, it seemed to be completely gore free. "Ouch!" They both screamed. Madam Spannel took no notice at all of this and only pointed at the two white, soft, shiny pairs of wings in front of the two girls.

Coco bent over and passed Luna her pair of wings. They put the little sticky-out parts into the holes in their backs, -Luna struggled with this seeing as she had a broken arm- and Coco and Luna felt as though they had an extra arm or leg!

They flapped the wings about enthusiastically for a few moments until Madam Spannel snapped, "Right! Everyone into launch position, immediately!" A rush of fear ran through the heads of Coco and Luna. The rest of the class lined up behind a silver bar at the foot of the course, Luna and Coco copied, they all bent down, the two girls still copying everyone else's actions. There was silence. It lasted for almost an entire minute. Madam Spannel walked behind them and raised five fingers in the air.

"Five!" she shouted,

"Four!" Coco looked rather nervous.

"Three!" She bit her lip in anxiety.

"Two!" Luna could hear her breath.

"One!" Coco fell back as the class burst upwards into the air. Luna only noticed this as she reached the first obstacle, she heard Coco crying loudly and Madam Spannel screaming at her. She flew back to find Coco and Madam Spannel standing in front of each other.

Sending spit flying over Coco's head, Madam Spannel yelled, "Detention is where you'll be flying right off to if you do not take this test immediately after everyone has finished! Have I made myself clear?" Coco nodded and wiped her eyes on her cardigan. "Right, now not a single *peep* from you Miss Wheezleberry. Copper, go! Unless you want to join your friend." Luna went into 'launch position', looked back at Coco with an awkward smile and flew to the very first obstacle. It was a set of pointed rooftops of what was supposed to be a city. She found this rather simple, even watching Skye Macdonaldson bang a different part of her body on every rooftop.

Next, was a minute volcano. It had a small cloud of smoke arising from the top so Luna thought it would be alive. She thought "Up, *go up!*" And she avoided it quite smoothly.

Thirdly, it was the Puddlefly. She flew further down so she could see how deep it was for Coco and she realised it was as deep as your average lake. *Luna* crossed it perfectly, unlike Skye Macdonaldson, who fell head first into the water and had to be pulled out by her friend Anna.

Finally, quick sand. Luna flew over it absolutely fine but along the way saw strange things like shoes, socks and even a pair of trousers being absorbed. Once she had finished, her and some other finishing students walked back to where Coco was in launch position.

"Three!" Madam Spannel yelled.

"Two!"

"One!" Coco shot upwards before falling down again. The class had expressions of both shock and laughter. "Shut up guys!" Luna screamed at them. Madam Spannel looked at her but said nothing. Coco went bright red and shot upwards again. She was only using one wing for a moment but she got both working again.

On the rooftops she lost a shoe and looked back to see if she had failed, but everyone just gave her dirty looks, except Luna, who crossed her fingers in front of her face.

Coco turned around and flew to the volcano where her other shoe was burned to crisp and she was just left with her long white socks. She stopped for over a minute before flying over to the Puddlefly. Jasmine, through the crowd of students, threw what looked like a small slimeball, into the air. She made a scrunched up face as it soared through the air towards Coco, and it started changing shape until it took form of a roll of sellotape. It sped to Coco and tied her wings together! Luna gasped in horror and looked around determinedly until she saw a basket of the slimeballs. "Aha!" She whispered. She ran over and picked out five or six of them. Before running back she threw one, "Cake, no. Bear, most definitely not. Hat, nope. Jacket, nope. Saw, nope. Scissors, no, actually yes!" The slimeball once again changed shape and became a pair of scissors that flew right through the sellotape.

Jasmine threw another which formed into sellotape. Luna through another, which turned into scissors, *sellotape, scissors! Sellotape, scissors! Sellotape, scissors!*

"Copper, Mundelio, detention, immediately." Madam Spannel yelled at the both of them. She marched over and grabbed their arms. Whilst she marched them inside Luna and Coco both smiled at each other as Coco got surrounded in people congratulating her. It made them both smile. (Coco and Luna that is, not Jasmine).

Madam Spannel marched Luna and Jasmine to a tall door, and opened it up to reveal an extraordinary room. There were glass cases around the walls with different shapes and sizes and colours of wings displayed inside them. One of the walls was a stained glass window, in front of it was a desk. Which had a sign noting, Arthur Borwung Whitesheild Rogererare. On the desk there was photographs of older fliers in pure gold frames and stacks of paperwork. And there was Rogererare, writing down something on a piece of paper.

"Oh, I wasn't expecting any visitors in the first month of term. What can I help you with?" He said.

"I caught these two using Superbios sir." Madam Spannel mumbled.

"Hmmm." Rogererare said softly. Madam Spannel dropped the two girls. "Ouch!" Luna yelled as she fell to the ground and her broken arm clicked. Madam Spannel went and stood in a corner and pretended to be rather interested in her left hand. The girls sat politely in front of Rogererare's desk.

"Well girls, since this is your first detention I am only asking you to dust my glass cases. Although, if anything possibly goes wrong then Miss Lulu Spannel will take over your detention in *her* office." He handed them both a duster and a bottle of washing liquid. They stood up and walked to the first couple of cases.

Only, on Luna's first case Jasmine said meanly, "Oh come *on* Copper, you better do better if you don't want to get detention with Cruella. Ugh! Get on with it!" Luna angrily shoved her duster to the glass, although, a little too roughly. It went completely through the glass! The wings fell like dominos. Rogererare let out a mighty yell although Madam Spannel let out a snigger.

"Merlin's Beard! No! Do you two know that those were some of the most famous fliers in histories wing fittings! Lulu Spannel! Take them, take them now!" Madam Spannel made a straight face again and gripped Luna and Jasmine by the ears and dragged them to a low-roofed room lit by a single air vent on the roof. On the 'desk' there was a sign saying Lulu Crochea Spanel.

CHAPTER THREE: DETENTION, AND A DEADLY DISRUPTION

Madam Spannel sat down on a comfy armchair and said, "Right! As your head teacher cannot do your detention, I will be doing it. We can do the easiest of punishments or the worst of punishments. What would you like?"

Jasmine dumbly replied, "Who cares?" Madam Spannel gave her a nasty look in a don't-you-dare-talk-to-me-that-way sort of way.

"Alright, ah. Ok. This is a punishment I've been doing for fifty years." Before they knew it they were hanging outside the window on a chain and upside down.

"Great move Copper." Jasmine said savagely, "I always had a bad feeling about you, especially once you started hanging about with that, what's her name? Er... Cooper?" She spat.

"It's Coco, and I'll have you know that she is great. You'll see. *I* promise. "Replied Luna sharply.

"Oh really Copper, well you can't even dust a stupid wing case, never mind make *decent* friends." Luna gave her a nasty look. "Silence!" Madam Spannel squealed and her long pointy fingernails dragged across the blackboard as she said it.

After about fifteen minutes Coco was walking by, wearing her glossy white practice wings and stroking Brownie's neck.

"Coco!" Yelled Luna. Coco looked around in fright. "Coco! It's me! Luna! Help!"

Coco looked up and gasped. She shot upwards until she was floating in front of Luna.

"Oh. Copper. Your *perfect* friend is here to rescue you! Wow! You're a legend Wheezleberry!" Jasmine said sarcastically with a smirk.

In a rather high-pitched voice, Coco squeaked. "What do I *do*?" When Luna opened her mouth to speak Coco yelped, "Wait a sec!" She flew away and returned with Louis. He was incredible at flying! He came speeding towards Luna and did hoops and nose-dives along the way! (Which were not a simple thing to learn). He was now floating a few centimetres away from Luna. Without a word his practice wings began moulding like a Superbio! Until they looked as though there were knives attached to them both!"

He twirled like a ballerina and his sharp wings cut the chain that Luna was tied to, in half! She was falling at high speed, protecting her broken arm. Louis dived after her and managed to grip her non-broken arm. She sighed in relief and let go. She laid down on the soft freshly-cut grass and Louis jogged over, trying to catch his breath.

"Wow! Louis! How are you *so* good at flying! Yelled Luna.

Louis replied, "Well, James is a flying coach for the Skywell Australian Dance Team, so I get quite a lot of practice. Luna and Coco both said "Who's James?"

Louis replied, "He's my guardian. On New Year's Eve 2015 there was a fire at the restaurant we went to. My sister Eve and I were the only ones who could reach a fire exit. I'm not sure exactly what happened but I do know that Eve, James and I love each other very much."

It occurred to Luna that she had more of a connection with Louis then she had thought. It was kind of nice to have someone around her who was also an orphan.

To change the subject, Luna mumbled, "So how old is Eve?"

Louis stared at her and said, "Well she had a birthday two weeks ago so she's... Nine? Yes nine. She was only four when the fire occurred, I was six."

Before anyone knew what was happening, they were in an emotional group hug. Although, it wasn't the type of group hug you'd get any old day. Coco and Luna could both feel something wet pouring down Louis's back. It was *blood!*

"Oh my! Oh my god Louis! You're... You're... You're bleeding!" Coco screamed. "Oh no." Louis whispered. He walked apprehensively out of the hug and flew away.

"What's up with him?" Coco asked with her eyebrows raised. Luna shrugged.

"I'm not sure." She answered, "But that scratch looked like it was from some sort of monster. Do you know of any?"

Coco thought for a few moments and eventually answered her friends' question, "Well... It could be a werewolf... But it could be a Yeti or a Comporatora-" She was interrupted rudely by Luna.

"*Comporatora?*" She asked with a look of confusion.

Coco looked at her in astonishment. "Well, yeah? She said. "I'm not sure exactly how it works but, I'm pretty sure that once human blood touches a Comporatora the owner of the blood will begin changing into one or something. If it was one that 'attacked' him, then he could be in *serious* danger." Luna opened her mouth to speak but Coco continued, "Lady Gatherhow will probably know about them more than I do. Do you reckon we should ask her?"

Luna nodded, but shrugged. "I guess so. But do you know where her classroom is?"

"Of course! Don't you remember! It was where the beginning of term party was, at the *very* beginning of the year. You *must must must* remember that!" Coco yelled at her.

Luna shook her head, "No. I started in the hospital wing."

Coco rushed a violent shade of scarlet, "Oh. Well, er, you didn't miss a *lot?* And plus, all of the fifth years and sixth years had hidden whiskey in their bags so it was *wild.* Now I think about it again, I wish I hadn't gone." She looked embarrassed. Luna smiled fakely as Coco quickly changed the subject. "Any... Anyways, do you want to go and ask Lady Gatherhow about Comporatoras now?" Luna nodded and followed Coco.

They stopped in front of a short, chubby woman wearing grey semi-circle glasses and she had short black hair. She looked like one of those people who had a constant cheery grin.

The lady said, "Oh well hello Miss Wheezleberry, who have you brought along here?

Coco replied, "Oh this is Luna, Luna Copper."

Lady Gatherhow's eyebrows raised, "Oh! You must be the Luna Copper everyone's been talking about. You do know that you were an extremely brave and *loyal* girl, coming face to face with that Barney Bubwul. What may I help you girls with?"

"Well, Miss. We were kind of hoping that you would give us some information about Comporatoras." Coco saidd nervously.

"Oh well girls, that's really something you should learn about *next year*. It can be a very traumatising topic. Are you sure you want to learn about them? And, if I may ask, why do you *want* to learn about them?" Asked Lady Gatherhow kindly.

"Well, we. Were, umm. We, er... Were, we were. We need information because we are helping a second year with their studies." Coco said quickly. She hadn't seemed to of convinced Lady Gatherhow.

"Well, who may this student be Miss Wheezleberry?" Lady Gatherhow replied. Coco froze. She tried to think of a second year but only could think of one. "Mae Stooper." She said hurriedly. Lady Gatherhow stared at her for quite some time before replying confusingly, "But Miss Wheezleberry. Mae is *top* of the class. I just simply don't understand how she could possibly need help with Beasts and Creatures of the Forests class."

Luna was listening very intently indeed, but she was confused. "Umm. Sorry to interrupt, but er... Lady Gatherhow? I thought you taught Wingcare and Maintenance class?"

Lady Gatherhow gave her an even wider grin, "Oh I do honey, it's just, when you go into second year I will *also* teach Beasts and Creatures of the Forests class." Luna nodded.

Coco eventually got to answer Lady Gatherhow's question, "Oh well, Miss, She... She... She wanted us to help her because... She, didn't want to put her reputation down even though she needed help. And she asked us to do it because... Because she didn't want to ask someone in her year in case they laughed at her."

Lady Gatherhow smiled kindly, "Alright, since it's for a kind deed I'll tell you about them. Ok?" The girls looked hopefully down at her. "Ok girls, a Comporatora is a dangerous creature that can only be found in the imagination, although, if you put too much thought into it. It can *seem* real, and if you go near one, in the imagination, they will aim to scratch you around your back. If they do, the human they attacked will become the next Comporatora, which can then be found in any flier in the worlds mind. The human who the Comporatora was controlling will be set free into their human body, but they would have missed out on a lot of their life. They can all look different, but once their around for a while, they may start to look a bit sickly. They will have two eye sockets, but only one eye, they will walk on two legs, they have devil horns, their teeth are like knives, and they have one tiny fluttering wing and one humongous one. They will have the growl of a bear, but are as fast as a cheetah. You have to be careful how much you think about them because they can hurt you."

Coco gasped and Luna gulped.

Lady Gatherhow looked at her flying watch, which was constantly fluttering around her head. "Oh dear! Girls, you've got to go to Sir Davies classroom, now! It's your last lesson of the day! I'll show you the way." The girls jumped and ran after her.

"Here." Lady Gatherhow said as she motioned the girls into a classroom with children sitting at desks and a man at the front. He just looked normal, except from the moustache he had which was black and wider than his face.

"Why hallo! Mademoiselle's! Welcome! To our classroom! Take a seat mademoiselle's, take a seat!" He said, Lady Gatherhow left the room and Coco and Luna sat down, laughing. "Is that all of my students? Ok, ok!" He laughed as well. "Ok I am Sir Davie. I hope you enjoyed that, *funny* accent! I am your Wing Painting teacher this year! Welcome to Winged Beauties!" Luna spotted Louis who appeared to be hiding in the very back seat of the back row of the classroom. He was avoiding eye contact. "This is your first lesson with me! So I thought I would give you a fun, but important assignment this time." Said Sir Davie. Luna had stopped looking at Louis now and was paying attention to her teacher. "This assignment is one that could *possibly* be used all over the world! My assignment is, to find something from the non-flier world, and attach it to your wings to communicate with other fliers when flying. This is relevant to my class because, once we have found the perfect thing we will be painting our wings. Now I'd like you to find a partner, and discuss what you're going to do. Then, after the lesson you will take a cloning juice tub, and one person from each pair will go, clone the items they want twice, one for both of you, and fly back to your partner, where you will work on your project. I would like this done in twenty-four hours please. Begin."

Luna and Coco faced each other. "Is Louis ok?" Coco asked worryingly.

"Coco, he seems fine just now, let's focus on the assignment first, *and then* deal with that, ok?" Luna replied. Coco nodded.

"Can you *please* go, because I've never been in the non-flier world before and you have?" Coco said anxiously. Luna smiled and nodded. Coco whispered, "Yes!" Then she loudly said, "So what're you going to get?"

"Dunno." Said Luna blankly.

"Well, what did you use when you were in that world?" Coco asked coolly.

"Well, we did use phones and iPads and stuff. I could get my old one and clone one for you!" Luna answered excitedly. "Sir! Sir Davie!" She said. Sir Davie walked over.

"Yes?" He asked.

"Can Coco and I have our cloning juice tub please? I think we are ready." She said as Sir Davie smiled and handed her a tub of cloning juice. She smiled back and put it in her pocket. "Thanks." She and Coco ran off and went to the grounds once more.

"Remember. In your old house, clone your phone, bring them both back. Ok?" Coco reminded Luna. She nodded and put on her practice wings, went into 'launch position' and flew away.

As she flew over her old house she landed and saw the glaring light of the TV in the living room. She gulped and opened the door silently. She stepped on a floorboard in front of the stairs and the TV stopped. Was it a coincidence? She thought. But when Alex opened the living room door she noticed it wasn't a coincidence.

"Alex, please Alex, please. Don't tell them I'm here. Please." Luna begged her cousin, who smiled and closed the door. The TV went back on so Luna knew Alex had, for once, stood up for her. She hurried upstairs and into her 'bedroom', grabbed her phone, poured the cloning juice onto it and another one arose from her floor. "Yes!" She whispered as she picked them up and placed them in her pocket along with the empty tub.

She opened her window and was about to fly out of it when she heard a tiny voice.

"I love you, you love me,

I like nice hot yummy tea,

You are kind, don't I know,

Your nice bow is quite a show."

She looked back to see her small fluffy dog teddy sitting on her old mattress. He was the only thing she had left of her parents. He sang that song anytime you rubbed his nose. She ran back and gripped him tightly as she flew out of the window. She listened to that song the entire way back to school.

Once she got back she met Coco in her dormitory, who stared at her cuddly dog.

"You're not allowed teddies here!" She said.

"Wait what!" Luna said, and she gripped her cuddly toy closer to her. (Which was actually called Toffee.) "I'm keeping him anyways!" She yelled and she hid Toffee under her bedsheets. Coco giggled.

"I got the phones!" Luna shouted. It echoed around the room.

"Oh!" Coco yelled. Which also echoed around the room. "Let me see!" Luna took the phones out of her pocket and gave Coco one of them. "*Wow!*" She whispered.

"Now go to the app settings ok?" Luna said whilst pointing to it on her phone. Coco eventually managed. "Now create an account." Luna said whilst talking Coco through how to type her name and date of birth. "Now press the little circle on the phone at the bottom." She said as she, once again, pointed to the home button. Coco did. "Now you see that little speech bubble at the bottom of the screen?" Luna pointed to the messages app. Coco nodded. "Well, press and hold any other app and press the delete button at the top corner of every app apart from that one." Coco didn't understand so Luna did it for her. "Now, I've never used messages before, I used the school app that my non-flying school used to use so go into the messages app." Coco clicked it. "Now make a name." Coco just did, 'Coco Wheezleberry'. Luna did 'Luna Copper'. Just for easiness. "Now type these numbers into that box. That's my phone number. Send me something." Luna said. Coco did.

[Coco Wheezleberry] Hello!

"Good!" Luna said. That came through! Now I'll send you something!" Coco smiled.

[Luna Copper] Hi!

[Coco Wheezleberry] I love these phones!

[Luna Copper] I know! They just have to win! No one can get something cooler than this!

[Coco Wheezleberry] Wait I'll go outside! See if it works when I'm further away! Do you reckon I should?

[Luna Copper] Sure! Why not? :)

[Coco Wheezleberry] Wait! Huh? How did you do that little person?

[Luna Copper] Oh. That's called an emoji. Go to the emoji button at the side!

[Coco Wheezleberry] :) :) :)

[Luna Copper] Haha!

[Coco Wheezleberry] Ok, I'll go outside. Just a minute!

[Luna Copper] Ok! See you in a minute!

Coco wheezleberry went offline

Coco wheezleberry went online

[Coco Wheezleberry] Ok! I'm outside! Can you see this?

[Luna Copper] Of course! :)

[Coco Wheezleberry] These are so cool, but they're so different from the mail I'm used to! And it's so quick! I'm in love with it. It's like instant! :) :) :)

[Luna Copper] I know! Just DON'T drop it! I'll have to buy you a new one if you do, and they are expensive!

[Coco Wheezleberry] Oh no! I wouldn't dare!

[Luna Copper] Thank goodness!

[Coco Wheezleberry] Come outside! It's very refreshing out here. Oh! I just noticed! I can see the time!

[Luna Copper] Er... Duh!

[Coco Wheezleberry] It is 10:11 PM!

[Luna Copper] Yup! Ok! I'm coming!

[Coco Wheezleberry] YAY :)

Luna copper went offline

Coco wheezleberry went offline

Luna ran outside to where Coco was sitting on the bench. "Coco!" Coco jumped. She ran over.

"They are so cool Luna!" Coco burst out excitedly. "I love them! Where did you get them? I'll ask my mum if I can have another one, and another, and maybe one more!"

Luna replied, "I got them from the phone store near my old house. I could show your family the way from here to there some time if you'd like?"

"Oh yes please! I would love that!" Coco yelled.

Luna replied. "Do you want to change your name to something more exciting? I'll do it too!"

"Sure! Can I change it to... Umm, what should I change it to Luna?" Said Coco. Luna shrugged.

"I'm going to go inside though, it's getting quite cold." Luna said.

"Right behind you." Said Coco casually.

When they got inside, they went to their dormitories but they texted for a while.

[Coco Wheezleberry] How do I change my name?

[Luna Copper] Go out of my contact and go to, 'Me' then go to your name and type your new name.

[Coco Wheezleberry] Ok, hold on.

[Luna Copper] Ok.

Coco wheezleberry changed the username to BrownieTheCwinger

Luna copper changed the username to ToffeeTheTeddy

[ToffeeTheTeddy] Nah! I think it was better when we were just Luna Copper and Coco Wheezleberry.

[BrownieTheCwinger] Most definitely!

Browniethecwinger changed the username to Coco Wheezleberry

Toffeetheteddy changed the username to Luna Copper

[Luna Copper] Ah, much better!

[Coco Wheezleberry] Yes. We weren't supposed to use these unless we were flying, right? Anyways, let's let ourselves away with it for tonight.

[Luna Copper] Hmm. Yeah! Sir Davie won't mind. He seems SO nice!

[Coco Wheezleberry] Nah! He doesn't care. I'm so worried about Louis. Do you reckon he's alright?

[Luna Copper] I don't know. It definitely seemed like a Comporatora scratch though, right? I mean, it was in the exact place on his back that Lady Gatherhow said. But it doesn't make sense! Why would he be thinking about Comporatoras? We don't even have proof that he knows about them yet! Let's hope it was just a Yeti or something. : (

[Coco Wheezleberry] Yeah. I guess you're right.

[Luna Copper] : (

[Coco Wheezleberry] This is probably the wrong time to be asking but, do you reckon he already has a date for the Christmas dance?

[Luna Copper] COCO!

[Coco Wheezleberry] Sorry, sorry. I just, I just, Ugh, what am I saying.

[Luna Copper] Well, it is in two days so I wouldn't be surprised if he has been asked or if even he's asked someone. Don't get your hopes up but you can try tomorrow. I have no idea who I'm going with. If he says yes can I just hang around with you guys? If he says no then we can go as friends.

[Coco Wheezleberry] Yes of course you can! I suppose I could ask him tomorrow! AHH I'm so nervous now! Thanks Luna! : /

[Luna Copper] Sorry : (

[Coco Wheezleberry] It's fine, although, it is 11:33 so we should probably get some sleep before tomorrow's presentation.

[Luna Copper] Yeah.

[Coco Wheezleberry] Goodnight ZZZ

[Luna Copper] Goodnight ZZZ

Coco wheezleberry went offline

Luna copper went offline

Once Luna awoke on Thursday, she sat up quickly. She was very excited about the things that were going to happen that day. Firstly, Coco was going to ask Louis to the dance! Secondly, they were going to have to do their presentation about the phones in front of Sir Davie. It was also Christmas day, and finally, they had to pick out an outfit for the dance! She jumped out of bed and grabbed her phone immediately.

Luna copper went online

[Luna Copper] Hi Coco! It's our big day! And, just to remind you! YOU'RE GOING TO ASK LOUIS TO THE DANCE! Merry Xmas :)

Once around half an hour had passed, of which Luna had gotten fully dressed, brushed her teeth, and fed Glee, Coco awoke, and replied.

Coco wheezleberry went online

[Coco Wheezleberry] Yes.

Coco wheezleberry went offline

This wasn't nearly as enthusiastic as Luna had thought it to be, but she thought it would do. She ran downstairs excitedly to meet Coco. Who had been holding a bucket of glossy black paint and looking at it with her mouth open. "Hello! Merry Christmas Coco! What is that?" Said Luna, looking at the bucket of paint in Cocos hands.

"It's enchanted wing paint! It makes it like, forty times faster!" Coco screamed.

Luna gasped, "Wow! Who's it from?" Coco reached into her pocket and gave Luna a small, crumpled piece of paper. It read.

Dear Coco.

I wanted to wish you a Merry Christmas! I thought this ought to help you with your Winghinging class. It is the black version, sorry, I would of gotten the white. But I'm afraid they only had black and brown. It times it by forty. The most powerful version of the type.

I dearly hope your schoolwork is going well, and please may you tell me about the new friends you've met there. It's a wonderful school, Winged Beauties.

My work is going well. I sold seven packets of speed tablets to a nice elderly woman. Who gave me twice the price!

Please tell me that Madam Spannel isn't nagging you on. Mum says she is. But I think (and hope) that it is only a random guess. Probably, you know mum. Making up stuff all the time. You better be looking after Brownie, Ryan will go nuts.

I hope your well.

Rachel x

Luna handed it back, and said, "Rachel seems nice. You're so lucky. What did your parents give you?" Coco pointed at a small, knitted pair of socks. Which were a violent shade of yellow. There was a small strip of paper sitting next to it, which Luna scanned her eyes over.

Dear Coco,

Merry Christmas darling. We hope you like your gift. Your mother knitted them specially.

We love you,

Love, Mum and Dad XOX

"That's nice, I guess" Said Luna nervously.

"Not if you have two pairs of each colour of the rainbow." Said Coco disgracefully. Luna laughed.

She noticed a small pile of boxes under the tree in the main hall, all with notes saying 'Luna' on them. She squealed and ran over, picked them all up, and ran to Coco.

"Wait, what's that note, you know, the one without a parcel?" Coco asked. Luna picked up a small note.

To, Luna.

Merry Christmas. Grandma and Grandad didn't want me to write to you. But I did. Maybe you're not so bad. I'll be leaving soon because mummy and daddy are back from London in a few days. I couldn't get to the shops, so I couldn't buy you a present, but I wanted to write a note.

From, Alex xxxxx

"Alex wrote to me?" Luna thought. But she kept the note none the less. Next Coco told her to open a package. It was wrapped in pure white wrapping paper and had a pink bow on top. There was a letter attached to it.

Dear Luna,

Merry Christmas, I was wondering why a pair of wings arrived at my door tonight to take my present, but Miss Klark told me about the, 'School' It was an honour to teach you. I hope you enjoy this gift.

From, Mrs Artson Xx

"Who's Mrs Artson?" Asked Coco.

"She was my old school teacher." Said Luna kindly as she opened the parcel up to reveal tiny little cupcakes sitting neatly on a tray. "Aww." Said Luna. Next, she opened a letter attached to the tiniest package of all.

Dear Luna,

Merry Christmas. Sorry, my pen is running out of ink. I so wish I knew what school you went to. Was it St Marigolds? Balta High? We all miss you so much. Hey! I don't know if I imagined this, but a blue thing came to my house today and it's waiting outside for this package. Please come over to my house soon. I miss you so.

From, Lulu xoxoxoxoxoxoxo

Coco looked at Luna with confused eyes. "She was my friend at my old school." Luna explained as she opened the package to reveal another box. When she opened this box, there was a bracelet in it. It had been clearly made out of Lulus friendship bracelet kit, but Luna slid it onto her wrist and smiled. The last package was a soft one. It had a long letter attached. But instead of noting 'Luna' it noted 'Private, To Luna Copper'

She opened the package first, it was a winter coat. Blue, with a white ribbon around the waist. Then she read the letter.

Dear Miss Luna Copper,

Merry Christmas, I suppose you know your way around the school by now? Am I correct? If so, then would you please meet me, meet me in the basement. Bring nothing, not even Miss Coco Wheezleberry.

My identity should not be a question you should ask yourself, the real question is, why do I want to meet? Well, I will not give any more information than needed, but I believe I have some explaining to do. By no fault of your own, I have been 'watching' you, not in a scary way. But over your lessons, to see how you're getting on.

Once you meet me, you will understand why and how I've been doing it.

I would like to meet you at midnight, on Sunday. I am someone who you believe to be gone, but I am not. I will never be. If, on Sunday, I am not visible. Then it is because I go without a body, or even a soul. However, my step brother does. He will also be there.

Please agree to this offer. If you don't, you'll regret it.

Good day.

"Coco, look!" Yelled Luna to Coco, who was looking at the tree sleepily. "Coco!" Coco looked round. "What?" She said. "Look!" Said Luna. She pointed to the paper, but it had gone blank. Coco patted Luna on the back, she was worried about this now.

"But... But Coco I, I swear... It... It was there!" Said Luna angrily as Coco helped herself to a cupcake.

"Maybe you should lie down for a while Luna, maybe you didn't get enough sleep or something. Just, just go for a quick nap, then we can go and do our presentation." Said Coco, sounding concerned.

"No! I don't need a nap! We'll, we'll go do our presentation, now! Or, I dunno. Just, I'm not taking a nap! And anyway, I'm getting my cast off very soon" Luna yelled.

"Ok, ok. Well. Go put your presents in your dormitory, I'll do the same. Then go get your cast off. Then we can do our presentation, ok?" Said Coco, calming down more now. They both ran upstairs and put their presents in the dormitories. Luna hurried to the hospital wing, where Mrs Penny was waiting for her. Without a word, she tugged at the cast a few times, until it came, clean off. Then she motioned Luna to the door, where she ran out. Then she ran downstairs again and met Coco under the tree in the main hall.

Once they had reached the classroom, they realised that they were the only ones in there, apart from Sir Davie, who was sweeping the floor.

"Why hello? You two are early. Just go and sit down. The class will be here soon." He said, and the girls sat down, got comfy and went over their presentation.

"Ok." Said Luna, "Should we redo what we were going to do?" Coco nodded.

Coco wheezleberry went online

Luna copper went online

[Luna Copper] Hi everyone!

[Coco Wheezleberry] Hello! We are going to be showing you phones!

[Luna Copper] These are things that the non-fliers use to communicate all over the world! They cost A LOT of money, but we can clone these ones. Then we can make them just like ours, where you can only text!

[Coco Wheezleberry] You can have countless contacts! But you need to make an account. We will attach them to our wings, and can use the twirling line move to keep typing!

[Luna Copper] It is instant, and will give you no added weight whatsoever! They are light! And, these types do not need charged!

[Coco Wheezleberry] Thank you for watching our texting method! :)

[Luna Copper] Yes! BYE XX :)

"It's *perfect*." Coco and Luna said simultaneously. The class had all arrived by this point, except, Louis wasn't there.

As if he knew why Louis wasn't there, Sir Davie introduced the first presentation. "Here is Skye Macdonaldson and Anna Rigmont with their, 'Postbox Drop'!" Skye and Anna stood up. Anna was holding a small red postbox, and Skye was holding some papers.

"Hi! This is a postbox Anna collected yesterday. We were thinking that when you're flying, you can drop a letter into this. We have made it so it goes to the dorm numbers only! We think it is the bestest most bestest thing *ever*!" Skye said in her usual girly voice. Everyone clapped.

Sir Davie said, "Next up, Jasmine Mundelio and Ruby Carneego, with their, 'Telephone Call'!" Jasmine and her friend Ruby stood up as Skye and Anna sat down.

"This is a telephone! It means you can hear another person's voice even if they are far away! You would attach it to the top of your fittings so that you can just answer anyone at any time! And, you can call anyone by doing a flying backflip!" Said Jasmine coolly as Ruby held the phone to her ear and pretended to be talking.

Everyone (except from Luna and Coco) clapped. Sir Davie announced a few more pairs of pupils until he called out Luna and Coco for their Texting Method. They walked silently to the front of their classroom, a shiver of nerves through their veins. They connected the phones to a flying painting and began their presentation. Once they had finished, everyone clapped loudly and the painting dissolved. They bowed and sat down again.

"I think that should bring us to the end of our lesson. I'll give these to the Winged Being Abuse Prevention Office today and President Feather will decide out of everyone in the entire flying world, whose presentation was the best. I'll get back to you guys tomorrow. Now. Enjoy the rest of your Christmas Day everybody! Goodbye for now." Sir Davie said.

Everyone left, and Luna and Coco scurried to Lunas dormitory.

"Phew, that's that over with. What do you want to do now? You could go find Louis, or we can go pick out our dresses." Said Luna, as she sat on her bed and began fluffing her pillow.

"Dunno, I guess we could go find Louis, you know, to get it out of the way." Coco replied casually, as she petted Glee.

"Ok. Well. I'll help you look. Maybe we can figure out why he has a Comporatora scratch when we're at the dance. Then do you want to go pick our outfits for tomorrow? Then we'll be free. I heard from Skye that it is an underwater theme. Like blues and greens and stuff." Luna replied as she put her pillow back. Coco shrugged and nodded.

They left the room and looked down the corridors, the kitchens, the classrooms, dormitory 731, (which, was Louis' dorm), and even the grounds, but he wasn't anywhere.

"There is only one place we haven't checked, and I was avoiding it." Said Luna.

"Where?" Coco asked dreadfully.

"The hospital wing. What if he *is* going into the mind of someone?" Luna whispered. Coco's eyes watered.

"Don't say that." She shivered. A tear poured down her cheek like a raindrop. Luna frowned, she hugged Coco tightly.

"Come on, we need to know." Said Luna quietly. They ran to the hospital to find one bed with its curtains closed. And Mrs Penny was running in and out hurriedly. When she opened the curtain to run back in, the girls noticed Louis lying on the bed, but he was fading, and fast asleep. "No!" They yelled and without thinking, they ran inside the curtains.

"Get out! Get out now! Get out! This could be serious girls! Get out!" Mrs Penny yelled in a vastly loud voice.

"Not until we know he's ok!" Coco yelled and she kneeled next to his bed. Luna did the same. Coco began to cry. Luna allowed her to cry on her shoulder, until Louis opened one eye. "Louis!" Luna yelled hopefully. Coco looked up.

"I'm sorry. I should have told you. It was a Comporatora, and I know who. June. June did it. June Stooper. The code is one, seven, four, nine, seven. I found out when I was studying. Use it, please. Use it to save me. I only have until one AM on Monday. Or else I'm gone." He said tiredly. Coco nodded. She never asked him about the dance because clearly this was more urgent, then Louis fainted. "Go!" Mrs Penny screamed. The girls took one look at her and ran away.

CHAPTER FOUR: A LARGE WIN AND DANCE PREPARATION

All of a sudden, when they were walking down the corridor slowly, they noticed Skye standing alone. She looked dazzled. Her eyes were wide open, and she was on her knees.

"Skye? Are... Are you ok?" Coco said nervously. Skye didn't answer, she just kneeled there. Coco looked at her and waved her hand in front of her face. "Hello?" She said. Once again, Skye didn't answer.

Luna had a sudden thought as she looked at Skye, "Wait! Coco, what if Louis is going into *Skye's* mind?"

"Yes! I mean, no! But you could be right! It would make sense, and I'm sure the person whose mind it travels to has no idea. Should we tell Mrs Penny?" Coco replied. Luna nodded. Coco let go of Skye and they ran to the hospital wing again.

"Mrs Penny!" Luna yelled as they ran down the corridor. "Mrs Penny! We know whose mind Louis is travelling to. Its, its, its Skye! Skye Macdonaldson! I swear!"

Mrs Penny ran hurriedly out of the curtains and over to the girls. "Ok. Girls, where did you see Skye?" She yelled quickly. Anna, who happened to be coming into the hospital at this moment for her allergy pills, overheard Mrs Penny talking and ran to the girls.

"What! Is, is Skye ok? Luna! Luna, Luna, Luna! Is Skye ok?" Anna squealed at Luna.

"I, I, I don't know Anna! But she needs to be seen!" Luna answered. Anna pulled at Mrs Penny's gown.

"Come on! Come on Mrs Penny! We need to find Skye *now!*" She screamed. Coco grabbed her arm and pulled her away from Mrs Penny, who seemed to be thinking deeply.

"Right girls! Coco, Luna, you get Skye and put her on the bed next to Louis' one. Anna, you wait next to the bed and calm yourself down. Get a drink of water and get your pills out of the cupboard, I will stay here and finish mixing Louis' medication. I think I can stop this." Said Mrs Penny. Anna got a drink from the fountain and got her pills, she sat down where her cheeks regained colour once more. Mrs Penny rushed into the enclosed cubicle. Luna and Coco ran to where they found Skye in the exact position they left her in.

They grabbed an arm each and tugged her to the wing and onto the bed. Anna stood up and tried to go onto the bed to wake Skye up.

"Woah! Woah! Anna! No! You can't do that! Get off! Get off!" Coco yelled as she and Luna had to hold her back as she cried.

"No! No let me! Please! I need to wake her up! Please! Please I'm begging you! Let me see her! Please! Please! I'll do anything! Please!" Anna screamed. Her face was either very sweaty, covered in tears, or covered in snot from her allergy of the type of wood the beds were made out of.

As much as this was painful for them to do, Coco and Luna both had to push Anna backwards so she fell awkwardly on her bottom. She ended up not noticing and still crying into her knees. Her pigtails hanging in front of her ears. Skye was still lying speechless on the bed. Her arms were at her sides like a soldier and her nice blue eyes were glistening with the chandelier light.

As Coco bent down with a few tissues in her hand to Anna's level, Luna looked over to see if Skye was alright, but she wasn't. Mrs Penny was nipping in and out of Louis' curtains. Getting more ingredients.

One of the times she nipped out for more strawberry seeds, Mrs Penny told the girls to go to bed and visit her in the morning so she could update them.

On the way to the 'Girls' corridor, Anna said, "Hey, can I maybe, well, get *one single innocent little* phone. Please?" Luna and Coco replied, "Fine."

They snuck into Sir Davies classroom and nicked one of the spare cloning tubs, cloned one phone, set it up for Anna specially, exchanged numbers, and Luna introduced them to a group chat called, 'CAL'. (It stood for Coco, Anna and Luna).

They said their goodbyes and walked to their own dormitories. Each and every one of them lay silently. They couldn't sleep, knowing what could happen by the morning, until Anna got the courage to actually send a message.

Anna Rigmont went online

[Anna Rigmont] Hi guys, if you don't reply its fine. But, I can't sleep. Can you guys?

Luna copper went online

Coco wheezleberry went online

[Luna Copper] No...

[Coco Wheezleberry] No. Me either, I'm scared for Skye and Louis, but who the heck is June?

[Anna Rigmont] What?

[Coco Wheezleberry] Louis said it was a girl, or Comporatora, named June Stooper. Wait! Sudden thought! Do you think she's related to Mae?

[Luna Copper] YES COCO! YOU'RE A GENIUS!

[Anna Rigmont] She could be. But, Mae goes to this school, so how would she be looking after this, June, girl?

[Luna Copper] Hmm... I dunno. Should we keep an eye on her tomorrow?

[Coco Wheezleberry] Sure... But it's the dance and we don't even have outfits! Although. If we wake up in the morning and Louis and Skye are ok, then they could help.

[Anna Charmer] Wait! I have exactly three dresses I couldn't pick from. That's such a coincidence! I can lend you each one if you'd like. Skye said she already has one, if she can go : (

[Luna Copper] Yes! That would be amazing! Right Coco?

[Coco Wheezleberry] Yes! What do they look like Anna?

[Anna Charmer] Well, one is blue. Very very very pale blue, with a normal blue design along the skirt. One is green, very very dark green, with a black design at the waistline. And the other one is coral yellow. Without any design at all. I was thinking I wanted the yellow one, but you guys can get first pick.

[Luna Copper] Oooh! The blue one sounds nice. You can have the yellow.

[Coco Wheezleberry] Yeah, Anna can have the yellow. Luna, you can have blue. They all sound nice so I don't mind the green one.

[Anna Rigmont] Ok. So I'm yellow, Luna's blue, and Coco's green. Cool. I'll drop them off in the morning guys.

[Coco Wheezleberry] Ok

[Luna Copper] Ok Anna.

[Anna Rigmont] I REALLY REALLY REALLY hope Skye can come, and Louis of course. :(

[Luna Copper] Yes. They'll be ok. I'm sure. Should I sneak to the hospital wing whilst everyone is sleeping? Or is that too cheeky?

[Coco Wheezleberry] YEAH! Go ahead Luna! I dare you!

[Anna Rigmont] If you want. PLEASE check on Skye too! It's almost one o'clock in the morning! Everyone is bound to be asleep by now.

[Luna Copper] Ok guys. I'll be back in ten minutes. I'll tell you guys EVERYTHING!

[Coco Wheezleberry] Ok x

[Anna Rigmont] Ok

Luna copper went offline

Luna put her phone down excitedly, wrapped her blanket around her body, opened the door, looked around, and tiptoed to the girls' corridor staircase. She scurried quickly down them, and ran to the hospital wing. She ran to Skye first, seeing as she was closest to the door.

Skye lay still. Her eyes were still open. Her body was still not moving. This gave Luna a bad feeling. Next she ran to Louis' enclosed cubicle. Mrs Penny was sleeping deeply in a chair. A notebook on her lap, and a pestle and mortar in her hand.

Luna peered innocently at the notebook in interest. Louis was still laid on the bed asleep. On the notebook was a bullet-point list.

- *Give Louis his finished medicine*
- *Check on Skye*
- *Make treatment for Anna's rash*
- *Give Olivia her stomach operation*
- *Repair Charlies leg*
- *Take my first nap this week!*

Luna noticed 'Give Louis his finished medicine'. Was it finished already? She looked at the mortar. The medicine looked ready, even though she *was not* a professional doctor. It was thick, and had mini lumps in the magenta colour. She thought for a moment, before deciding she was going to test it on herself before Louis.

She dipped her finger in it, and nothing happened. She dipped it in again, and nothing happened. For the last time, she tried it once more, and nothing happened.

"Ugh!" She thought. She slumped slowly down towards the door, until her feet decided to die. She stood awkwardly, trying to walk, but her body was literally attached to the floor.

All of a sudden, a boiling ball of fire flew down her throat. It went down to her chest. And replaced her heart with itself. As much as this hurt, Luna felt uplifted. She stood up tall. And ran back to Louis.

"I'm better! I'm better! I feel *so* much better. And I wasn't even sick! Ha!" She sang loudly.

As she approached, she immediately grabbed the mortar and touched Louis' lip to it. He sat bolt upright, his face slowly flushed back to life and he grinned at Luna with a confused but definitely 'Louis' look.

"Yay! He's so much better! I made him better! It is all because of me!" She sang giddily. She was extremely hyper, and deep down she knew it. Louis sat up straighter, grinning wider.

"I'm better! I'm better! I. Am. *Better!*" He sang. They sang and grinned until the sun began to rise through the window. They both ran back to their own bed's happily. Luna had completely forgotten that Anna and Coco were both sitting in bed worrying, waiting for an update.

Once the sun had completely risen. Anna ran to Coco's dormitory, where she found Coco on her bed with her head in her knees. Anna sat next to her and she looked up. They had both cried most of the night.

"Hi. What do you think happened to Luna! Why did she not reply?" Anna asked sadly.

"I dunno. Should we go to her dormitory and see what happened?" Coco replied, sounding depressed. Anna nodded. They ran over to dormitory 335. (Luna's dorm). And saw her sleeping on the bed. "Luna!" Coco yelled. They both ran to the sides of Luna and began shaking her.

"Ow! Oww! Stop! Stop that! Hey! I'm up I'm up! *Ouch*!" Luna yelled, shielding herself from the girls. Once they stopped. She continued, "Oh! Hey guys! Ouch! My head hurts. What happened?" Anna and Coco exchanged looks.

"I don't know! Why did you not update us on Skye and Louis though? We were *so* worried. Tell us! Now!" Coco said angrily. Anna nodded and frowned.

"Oh. Er... Oh! Oh yeah! Well. I had to test Louis' medicine so I took a few finger dips of that. And then I gave it to Louis and he, er, oh yeah! He woke up and then he went back to bed. There you go. You're all up to date." Luna replied sleepily as she rubbed the back of her head.

"Wait, really! You really cured him? Really!" Coco screamed excitedly.

"Uh huh. Well, I think so." Luna whispered. She turned onto her stomach and grabbed her phone.

"What're you doing?" Coco asked in a vastly irritated voice. "Why have you picked up your phone?"

Luna turned onto her back again and said, "Dunno. Just checking the group chat."

"Wait! If Louis is cured, does that mean, does that mean Skye will be ok too! Oh, and Luna. How much of that 'medicine' did you take? You seem kind of drowsy." Anna added.

"Hmm. Probably around a third of the mortar. Although, it was kind of rich. I feel kind of sick now I think about it again. I'm fine though." Luna answered. "Oh! Good point Anna, go check. In fact, I'll come too!" Anna smiled brightly, Coco sniggered in excitement, and Luna crawled out of bed. Got dressed, and stumbled out of the door with Coco and Anna.

Once they had reached the hospital wing, the realised that Skye's eyes were now closed and she was on her side. "Oh my! Is she, dead, or asleep?" Anna said worryingly. Coco looked confused. But Luna didn't.

"Come on guys! Let's try to wake her up!" She said, in a voice that made it seem as though this was a plan she had been planning all night.

"Of course!" Anna and Coco yelled, Coco banged herself on the forehead and Anna smiled. Anna took a deep breath and ran over to her friend. She pushed her gently. One of her eyes slowly began to awaken.

"Oh." She muttered. "Oh hi! I, I, I don't know, what, I don't know what, what, what happened, I, I just, I just felt sleepy or something, then, I, I, I fell over, or, I don't understand, I, I was, in some sort of, some sort of, thing, like, like op, optical, an, an optical illusion, or, yeah, I, I was in a, a, an optical illusion." Skye looked tired, and her hair was almost as messy as Luna's.

Anna stared, wide mouthed, and then decided to hug Skye. "I. I can't believe it! Your, you're ok!" She yelled excitedly.

Coco only just noticed a tear roll down Luna's cheek. She grabbed Luna's arm and pulled her to the corner of the room. "Hey, are you sane? Is my best friend sane now?" She said kindly. Holding Luna's shoulders.

"Yeah, I er, I'm sorry I didn't, didn't tell you guys last night. Today was, supposed to be, special. It's the dance. The dance to celebrate our seventh month here and, well, I've already ruined it." Luna replied, her eyes dull and her tears getting faster and faster.

"Hey, you haven't ruined anything. Not one thing. You have *saved* our friends. And the dance isn't until five o'clock. It's only seven in the morning. We have time. Lots of it." Coco replied.

"Oh, I know. But I still feel guilty. Very much so. And knowing that you forgive me, for some reason, makes it worse. Like I did it behind your backs. I, I'm so sorry." Luna turned away from Coco.

"Well. We're all tired. Maybe another couple of hours of sleep will do us all some good. Anna! Skye! I think we all need our own beds for a couple of hours longer. Maybe until nine? Then Sir Davie will tell us who won the competition. Then we should maybe try on our dresses? Then get our hair done and we might even squeeze in a little makeup. Don't know, but then it'll be the dance. Deal?" Coco recommended. Anna and Skye came over and Luna, Anna and Skye all said simultaneously, "Deal!"

They all ran back to bed. As Luna laid down on her bed, she noticed Toffee sitting silently next to her. She picked him up, held him close, and turned onto her side. She fell asleep in minutes, but had a strange dream. She was in a dark, enclosed room, with someone familiar. She couldn't recognise who it was, but felt stupid about not being able to. He was short, had long ears, a bald head, and he was wearing a pair of blood-stained trousers and a white T-shirt. Who was he? Who was he? *Who was he!* Luna felt claustrophobic, even though she had never experienced this before. She was walking silently down a staircase towards this man, but then she heard a voice, "Luna, Luna, Luna be safe. Please. All I ask of you, he is dangerous, he is dangerous! Watch out! *Watch out!*" It said. "What? Who are you? Why? Who is he? Tell me!" She was screaming. The small man took out a gun. He was pointing it at Luna. The voice said, "Before I tell you, bring her. All I'll say, bring her. Or else your present could be your future. And your future could end horribly, now, I am-" The voice blurred out.

"Luna! Luna! Wake up! It is nine o'clock!" Luna suddenly sat up and Anna and Coco were bent over her.

"Wait! No! Barney! That was Barney! Coco! You need to come! On Sunday! To the basement! You need to! Someone told me! I don't know who! But you need to!" Luna squealed as she burst up.

"What? Ok, I'll come. Whatever. But yeah! It's nine! Get changed! Sir Davie's about to announce the winner! We don't want to be late!" Coco yelled as she jumped around excitedly.

Luna took a moment to process everything that had just happened, but with some clarity, she replied, "Oh, yay, the winner, of course! Ok, and I'll get you on Sunday Coco. Hold on guys, turn around, I'm going to get dressed." Anna and Coco turned around and Luna changed into her usual blue top, black cardigan, blue tartan skirt, and long white socks. "Ok! I'm ready!" She yelled.

"Ok! Let's go see who won! Good luck to you guys, but I also hope I win!" Anna smiled. They all sniggered. On the way to the 'girls' staircase, they bumped into Skye.

"Oh! Hey guys! I'm feeling *much* better! Thanks. Let's go see who won!" She said happily. Downstairs they also bumped into Louis in the main hall. The five of them found seats near the front. Sir Davie was on the stage with some cards.

"Good morning everyone! I know this is a very special day for all of you. So, we will start in a few minutes." He said.

As more groups and pairs of people arrived, the hall got quite noisy. Although when Sir Davie began his speech, it all calmed down.

"May I get your attention please? Ok, we may begin. Firstly, President Feather would like to thank all of the following schools, for their entries in the competition. Carters Winged School for Flying Children, Winged Beauties Boarding School for Children with the Gift, Mr Chuckson's School for Talented Flying Boys, Madam Shoo's Boarding School for Young Female Fliers, Sir Mac's School for Flying Children, and Saint Molly's School for Flying Kids. He has sent these cards to me and all other school Wing Painting teachers. Now. For our school. Sorry, just let me find the card." The school pupils laughed, typical Sir Davie. "Right. Found it. Ok. Now for this school, he has received four hundred and seventy six entries. But he only gave us the top three in the school. All of which, coincidentally, first year students. In third place, I would like to award the medals to, Jasmine Mundelio and Ruby Carneego! Well done girls! Your 'Telephone Call' got one hundred and two votes!" Jasmine and Ruby stormed up to the stage. Katie and Jennifer, (Jasmine's two sixth-year friends), were clapping loudly. Sir Davie placed the two medals around their necks, and Jasmine stormed off of the stage, Ruby trailing calmly behind her.

"Ok. Second place. I would like to give the two trophies to, Skye Macdonaldson and Anna Rigmont! Good job girls! Your 'Postbox Drop' got one hundred and seventy two votes!" Sir Davie announced.

"Oh my goodness! Well done guys!" Luna yelled to Skye and Anna. Who looked shocked, and ran excitedly up to the stage, where Sir Davie handed both of them small, glistening, silver trophies, both of which had their names carved into them. They held them proudly, in the air then ran back to their seats.

"Now, for the moment you've all been waiting for. The first place winner! Now these two students were not only the worldwide winners, but they got over three hundred votes! Astoundingly, their project will now be used by every flier in the world! This is a massive achievement, so these two names will be engraved into a plaque for ever more. I am proud to announce, that, drum roll please." The entire school drummed on their tables. "Stop!" They all stopped and listened closely. Luna, Coco, Skye, Anna and Louis all held hands hopefully, "I am proud to welcome to the stage, Coco Wheezleberry and Luna Copper who's 'Texting Method' got three hundred and forty seven votes!"

Luna and Coco squealed as loud as possible and jumped in the air! "Oh my god! Oh my god! Oh my *god!*" Squealed Coco, "We won! We won! We *literally* won!" Luna squealed. They sprinted up to the stage where Sir Davie handed them a plaque which, engraved into it, said, 'COCO

WHEEZLEBERRY, 12. LUNA COPPER, 12. WINNERS OF WORLDWIDE COMPETITION'. Coco started crying with happiness. Luna was just speechless. Coco yelled, "Thank you!" and they bowed, walked off the stage, and hugged Anna, Skye and Louis.

Once they had gotten all of the physical excitement out of their systems, they ran to Anna's dormitory, where she had all three dresses laid out on her headboard.

"Oh, er, I need to go get *my* suit on, so, I'll see you ladies at the dance!" Said Louis, clearly wanting to get out of the room they were all going to get changed in. He left. The girls giggled.

"Oh! I'll go get my dress from my room, then we can all try them on. Ok?" asked Skye. Anna, Coco and Luna agreed, so Skye skipped off to get her dress. While she was gone, Coco and Luna helped themselves to a walk around the room. Anna's dormitory looked like a five star hotel room! It was mostly white but it had dots of gold here and there. Her bed was double and had a golden, woollen headboard.

Luna noticed Coco, looking very jealous of all of it. "Are you ok?" Asked Luna.

"Yeah, just, Anna's dorm is just so, so, so luxurious. Whereas, mine is just, just a big pile of wood and wool." She replied. Luna patted her on the shoulder and smiled. Coco smiled back.

Skye rushed into the room again carrying a large, fluffy, white dress. She blushed. "I... Just... Saw... Louis... He... Is... Wearing... A... Very, very, nice suit. He looks quite nice." She panted.

"Cool!" Said all of the girls simultaneously. Then they all giggled.

"Right ladies! I have also got beautiful, rented, wings for us all to wear to the dance, but don't let anything happen to them, my sister would *kill* me! Ok?" Anna said. Everyone nodded. "Ok. Well. I have moved stuff around in my wardrobe so that each of us can have a turn getting changed. Then, once we are all dressed up, I can help with you guys' makeup. Then we can do our hair. Who wants to go first?"

Coco raised her hand, "I can."

"Ok. Here's your dress and matching wings! It's very pretty!" said Anna, as she handed Coco the green dress and black wings. Coco hurried into the wardrobe and came out looking stunning. Her black wings were long, fluffy and thin. They were drifting gradually in the air, and her dress was just as Anna had described. It was very dark green with a black design at the waist.

"How do I look?" Said Coco nervously, "Do I look decent enough?" Everyone nodded and Coco sat on the bed.

"Ok. Should I go next?" Anna asked.

"Sure." Said Luna.

"Yeah?" Replied Coco.

"Yes ok. I kind of want to go last, so sure!" Answered Skye. Anna grabbed the yellow dress and yellow wings, and ran into the wardrobe. She walked out looking very nice. Her yellow wings were small, clear, and very thin. And her dress was solid yellow. She looked absolutely amazing.

"Wow!" The girls all said. "Thanks!" Replied Anna gracefully.

"Ok, so Skye, you want to go last? Ok then Luna, here is your dress and your wings." Anna said. She handed Luna the pale, blue dress and solid blue wings. She ran into the wardrobe, and also returned looking gorgeous. Her solid blue wings looked as though they were made of concrete. But they were thin and light. And her dress was extremely pale. Its design around the top and bottom was mythical and made her feel pretty.

"Does this look ok?" She asked.

"Of *course it does Luna*! You look amazing!" Anna screamed. All of the girls said, "Uh huh!" and Luna sat down as Skye ran into the wardrobe with her white dress and white wings. When she returned again her thin fluffy wings fluttered uncontrollably and her puffy white dress flowed gently with the air.

"Amazing!" They all yelled. Skye smiled, as Anna stood up and said, "Right! Makeup!" The girls got to their feet again, Luna looking intriguingly at Anna's pet. It was a kind of puppy and it didn't look magical at all. It looked like a baby German Shepherd, and its eyes were green, it was sitting contentedly on Anna's flower-decorated windowsill.

"Ok! Well, I think I know what themes of makeup would suit all of us. My mum is a makeup artist actually. I think Luna's makeup should most definitely be blue, because of her dress and wing colour. Coco's should probably be black, like a Goth. Skye, well, I think natural would go quite well, and I can maybe go with a yellow, orangish theme. Sound good? Then we can all use one of my hairbrushes." Anna said. Luna could tell she wanted this to go quite well. She, Coco, and Skye agreed with her.

Anna motioned Luna over to her white desk and sat on the soft stool. She stared at herself in the mirror for a few moments, before Anna walked in front of her, blocking the view. To Luna, this was quite relaxing, the brushes were very gentle, and Anna tried to come in from the side, so that Luna could see the other girls on the bed in her reflection.

After around ten minutes of having to sit still, Luna stood up and turned around. Not expecting this reaction, she watched as the girls' mouths opened and they gasped.

"What do I look like?" Luna asked, secretly hoping for another large answer. Only once she realised she wasn't getting one, she turned around and looked in the mirror. What she saw, made *Luna* gasp. Her lips were dark blue, her eyelids were blue, and her eyelashes were longer than usual.

"Do you like it? Or is it too much?" Asked Anna nervously. Luna was speechless, she just continued staring at herself in the mirror, jaw dropped. Once Anna had moved her gently to the cushion on the floor, she watched Coco and Skye have the same reaction to their Goth, and or natural looks. Anna seemed to be unnaturally fine with her look. She just stood up again and handed everyone a golden hairbrush.

Luna had no difficulty styling her hair. It was black and silky. She managed to put it into a neat pleat at the back of her head. Coco however, had much difficulty. Her hair was a bright shade of ginger, and was extremely tuggy and thick. The only up-do she managed to do was two buns on the top of her hair, her family had *not* had enough money to ever go to the hairdressers. Skye had the same amount of difficulty as Luna, seeing as her hair was wavy, brown, and thin. She ended up curling it even more, using a technique she learned as an older child, and leaving it down. Although Anna did a very complicated up-do she did made it seem easy, with her long, straight, blonde hair. She almost always had it in two tight pigtails.

Once everyone had complimented each other, Coco suggested, "Guys. Shouldn't we get to the East Hall? Its two minutes past five. And, Anna, Skye, don't you guys have *dates*? You wouldn't want them to leave, now would you? Let's go!"

"Oh! Yeah, er. It's not a, *date*... It's more of a, a, a friend, thing." Skye answered. She and Anna blushed.

"Ooh la la!" Luna and Coco said, in rather romantic voices. "Ooh!" Anna and Skye managed to keep their laughter inside, although they were only just smiling. They linked arms, reached for the doorknob, and waked to the 'girls' dormitory staircase.

As they arrived at the East Hall doors, they realised how much of a formal dance this was going to be for them.

CHAPTER FIVE : THREE IMPORTANT EVENTS

As they looked around, they met Louis.

"Hi. Do you like my suit?" he asked. The girls nodded.

They noticed the chairs were no longer wooden, they were white and fluffy stools, and the tables, were no longer large wooden ones, they were circular, with white glistening tablecloths upon. The windows were now opened completely and little fish tanks lay on the window sills. The floor had been covered in blue watery carpet and the chandelier was no longer there. It was replaced by a large shark, with what looked like fish-shaped candles in its mouth. It was rather dark, but it made a good atmosphere. Along the edges of the room there were more circular tables, each full of sandwiches, small sticks of cucumber and carrots, and bowls of salty crisps, Chris' Chocolate Cake Capsules, and strawberry mousse. There was also a gift shop, selling semi-speed cake for the flying, instant colour wing paint tubs, and randomised emotion smoothies.

"Ooh! I want to get a randomised emotion smoothie! They're only one pound each! Do you guys all want some?" Luna screamed excitedly.

"Sure!" answered Coco, Skye and Anna. "Why not?" Louis answered.

"Ok. Back in a minute." Luna smiled. She ran over to the gift shop, where she was greeted by Lady Gatherhow.

"Why hello dear! What may you like?" She asked kindly, with the usual happy grin that permanently stood upon her.

"Five randomised emotion smoothies, please." Luna replied, trying hard to have a happy grin alike her teacher.

"Ok dear, do you have five pounds? If not, you can give me three pounds and get six." Lady Gatherhow asked cheerfully.

"Er, yes, yes I do. Here you go Miss. I hope I can use the get six for that deal." Luna replied, as she took out three pounds from her pocket.

"Thank you, dear. I recommend keeping one in your pocket for tomorrow. They're quite expensive *usually*." Lady Gatherhow recommended.

"Ok. I will. Bye Miss. Thank you!" Luna said, as she hid a smoothie in her pocket and took the other five back to her friends.

"Here guys! Take your pick. Then we'll drink them on three." she said. Skye, Coco, Anna, and Louis all took a smoothie, opened it up, and waited for Luna to count. Once she had opened her smoothie, Luna excitedly said, "One! Two! Three!"

They all took large drinks, and waited for a few moments, before Skye interrupted the silence in their corner. "Guys! Ooh! That was nice! I wonder what emotion I got! Oh! Oh! I feel, I feel giddy! I can't stop talking! Aaah! Ooh! Anna! Anna! What did you get, what did you get! Ooh! Luna! What about you! Ooh! Coco! Louis! What did you guys' get-" She was interrupted by Madam Spannel, who had not dressed fancy, she had only changed from her black clothes, to navy blue clothes.

"Such noise, is not permitted in the hall. Miss Macdonaldson. If I hear it again, you will be locked in your dormitory for the rest of the night. Am I clear?" she snapped.

"Yes Miss. You are clear, haha! Oops!" Skye replied as she blocked her mouth with her hand.

"I think I got sad. I just feel down now, Luna, thanks a lot." Anna said randomly. "Ugh."

"Anna, oops. Sorry Anna, I. Ow! Anna I am so severely apologetic. I did not intend to damage your emotional health system. I only thought it would be something vastly enjoyable." Luna replied. Although she gasped afterwards. "Dear lord! What has occurred here? Why am I so largely intelligent? I can remember that the drinks we only just swallowed may only last for half of one hour. I may have gotten a rather intelligent emotion smoothie."

"Er, sure?" Coco replied. "Oh! I think I got coolness. I'm talking like someone cool. Like normal Coco, kinda." Coco said, in a 'cool' voice. "Anyway. Did you say that it only lasts for half an hour?"

As Luna went to answer, Louis interrupted, "Yes she did. Oops. Sorry."

Luna said. "Yes Coco, you are accurate.~"

"Yeah." Louis interrupted once more. "I, I, I, I, I, I don't mean, wait, what, I, huh, I must of gotten, like, some, like some sort of rudeness smoothie, or, or something."

"It's cool Louis. It'll wear off." Coco replied 'coolly'.

Once half an hour of dancing, karaoke, eating, and joking, had passed, the emotion smoothies began to wear off, and the clock chimed six o'clock. At this point, there was more karaoke, and Rogererare made a speech, "Alright. I dearly hope you all are enjoying your dance. Before we do our next round of karaoke, I would like to announce a large event that you can choose to do instead of the dance, if you would wish, once the karaoke, has finished. Now, most of you, would have met our Wing Picking teacher, Sir Davie, if I am correct. Now he has been researching the nearby locations around the school, and he was looking for two volunteers from year one, and two volunteers from year two, to go and fly to several different locations. This will take place from six thirty, and nine o'clock this evening, so you will be able to get back for the partner dancing, the flying show, and the midnight feast. You will not undo your hair or, if you're wearing any, makeup. Although you will have to change to suitable clothing for this length of time. May you raise your hand if you would like to take the time to go on this trip with our member of staff."

Many first and second years raised their hands, including, Luna, Louis and Anna. Rogererare looked closely, at who had put their hand in the air.

"Hmm." He said politely, "May, Luna Copper, Louis Lochsmith, Shannon Carneego, and Michael Barnumbio, please go on this trip?" Luna, Louis, Ruby's sister Shannon, and a random second year Michael, all stood up.

"I'll be back soon my friends, alright?" Luna whispered, as she, and Louis made their way to the stage, where Sir Davie handed them, Michael, and Shannon, all a backpack.

"Thanks Sir. I'll tell them what to get for the trip. Never you mind, we'll meet you at the front gates." said Shannon in an irritatingly perfect voice. Luna noticed the badge on her cardigan, noting, 'Perfect Proper Language Use, Head Ambassador'.

"Thank you Miss Carneego. You all have fifteen minutes to dress, and to pack. Shannon, you know what to pack. I'll meet you all at the front gates." Sir Davie said quietly. Luna, Louis, Michael, and Shannon nodded, and Shannon announced that they must follow her.

Once they had reached the West corridor, Shannon demanded, "We will all dress in the bathrooms, once you have changed into either a t-shirt and trousers, or a jumpsuit, you will all go into the dormitory and pack every single item on this list, into your backpack." She handed everyone a list of items that they would 'need' for this 'trip'.

- Some sort of water bottle
- Your copy of 'Birds and Other Non-Flying Animal Checklist Book' by Chad Copt
- Your new phone, that has been left in your dormitory, set up with your full name, attached to your usual wing fitting and filled with every school member
- Your animal healer. (IF ANIMAL FOUND HURT, MUST HEAL. ONLY ALLOWED TO KEEP ONE ANIMAL FOR ANOTHER PET IF SIR DAVIE IS NOTIFIED)

If any other item is needed for personal references, allowances can be made.

"Er, ok." said, Louis and Michael. Luna replied, "Ok my fellow chosen one." and grabbed her yellow jumpsuit out of her bag, and ran into the bathrooms to change. Once she had done so, she read the list over. She knew immediately that her water bottle was on her bed, she remembered seeing that book on her bottom shelf somewhere, she could most definitely work the phone and put her wings on. Except, she couldn't remember seeing an animal healer, although she remembered seeing a random box with something in it on her desk. She was extremely excited that she could perhaps get another pet, if she healed it.

Luna ran upstairs and into her dormitory, she grabbed her bottle, scanned the shelf and found her book, attached her wings onto herself, and grabbed a tin from her box, she read the back of it.

'Can be used on any animal, whether bleeding, freezing, burning, drowning, suffocating, or unconscious. Just feed it a drop of this water, and either keep it, or let it roam free.'

"Cool. Oh, I must have gotten the ten minute one. I'm back!" She whispered, as she packed all of these items into her bag. She ran downstairs, and met Sir Davie at the front gates, along with Shannon, Louis and Michael.

"Ok. Shannon had a typo. You are allowed to heal and keep, any amount of animals, as long as they are animals that can be domesticated, and are in one group. Now, we are going to the frozen lake first of all, and here, we are allowed to split up, although, if there is an emergency, text immediately. Now, follow me." Sir Davie said, as he shot upwards, and the rest of them followed.

As they landed tentatively next to a frozen, snowy area, Sir Davie nodded, and everyone ran away in different directions.

As Luna sat for a break, underneath a skinny tree, in the shade, she heard a few dying cat noises. She ignored it, and imagined herself making things up. She wrapped herself in her right wing, and rested on the tree.

A few moments later, she heard the meowing again, only it didn't sound like the three or four cats she heard before, it sounded like one cat, in deeper trouble. Luna swung her left wing in front of her, and on the phone, she looked for Sir Davie's contact. Once she had found it, she immediately texted him.

Luna copper went online

[Luna Copper] Hi Sir, am I allowed on the ice? I heard a few hurt animals coming from that direction.

Once a few minutes had passed, Sir Davie looked, and replied to, Luna's text.

Callum davie went online

[Callum Davie] Sure. Just be careful, you do not know how thin or thick it could be. And remember, heal the animal(s) by feeding it one drop of the water, and then use one of the fifteen provided blankets to wrap them up. One animal per blanket though, that's important. You can keep them if it's cats or dogs or ponies or BABY wild animals, which you can train when we get back. If it is

an adult, I'm sorry, but you can't keep it. Unless it is with it's baby. Make sure you can carry all of them.

[Luna Copper] Ok Sir. Do they need to get tests when we get back home? You know, to make sure of no diseases or something?

[Callum Davie] Well, we can test them, although in the tin you've packed. There should be a flying thermometer. You can throw it in the air and it'll circle each animal individually and you will be notified if any animal has anything bad.

[Luna Copper] Ok. If it does have something, how do we fix it.

[Callum Davie] Don't you worry about that, there's a cupboard in the staff room with all kinds of cures Mrs Penny has come up with.

[Luna Copper] Ok, bye! Xx

[Callum Davie] Ok hon, bye.

Luna copper went offline

Callum davie went offline

Luna swung her wings back behind her, and headed for the middle of the frozen lake. As she landed on a floating rock, she saw what had been meowing. She saw one tiny white kitten, with blue eyes, another one that looked exactly the same, except it had one ginger ear, and one completely grown, ginger cat, with blue eyes, who was holding the kittens behind its paws.

Luna walked slowly towards them, and petted the larger one on its head, it purred gratefully. She picked up the pure white kitten slowly, and got her tin out of her bag. She fed it one drop, from her finger, as asked. The kitten rubbed itself all over her stomach.

Next Luna threw the flying thermometer into the air and it circled the kitten. When it returned to Luna's hand, in giant green writing, it displayed the word, **HEALTHY**. Luna smiled, and took out a fluffy yellow blanket, of which she wrapped the kitten up, and placed it comfortably, in her bag.

Next, she picked up the other kitten, did the same steps, and the thermometer displayed the words, **FROSTBITE, CAN BE CURED WITH PURE DIAMOND MELTED LIQUID.** "Oh no!" Luna yelled. She immediately texted Sir Davie.

Luna copper went online

[Luna Copper] Sir Davie! Help! I found three cats, and one has Frostbite! Do I still wrap it up? And just get that diamond stuff when we get back.

Callum davie went online

[Callum Davie] It's ok Luna, just feed it one more drop. These are old, diamond melt CAN help, but it'll be fine with one more drop, now I'm busy hon, Shannon, has just snapped her wings in half by a tree branch.

[Luna Copper] Oh, ok. Thanks, bye. Xxxx

[Callum Davie] Goodbye!

Luna copper went offline

Callum davie went offline

"Oh thank goodness." Luna whispered to herself, in a way that if anyone saw her, they would think her a creepy spy.

She dipped her finger in the tub, and fed the kitten one more drop, then wrapped it inside a pink blanket, and placed it with the other kitten in her bag. As she reached for the adult cat, it began meowing and going on its hind legs to touch Luna's knee.

"What's up kitty?" Luna said, in a 'babyish' voice. The cat meowed once more, and ran to an open gap, in the ice. Luna only noticed something, when an unconscious, white, gleaming cat, floated from under the ice. "Uh! Oh, er, I'll get them, don't worry kitties." Luna said as she picked up the unconscious cat, she fed it a drop, and it's beautiful green eyes opened up. It yawned, and leaped to the ginger cat. As their tails wrapped around each other happily, Luna immediately knew that these two cats were in love, and the kittens were most likely theirs.

She fed the ginger cat a drop, and threw the thermometer around the white cat, of which it displayed, **WEAK**, although Luna had expected this. When she threw it around the ginger cat, it displayed, **HEALTHY**, she wrapped them both in two separate, green blankets, and placed them with their kittens.

She closed her bag, cautiously, leaving a tiny gap in the zip, so the cats could breathe, and she set off to the tip of the lake, where she met Sir Davie, Louis, Shannon, and Michael.

"Ok, now that we have all met, once again, would everybody please share what they have found, or healed and kept, please?" Sir Davie announced.

"Well, I was sitting, by the lake, and I was counting the fish I could see, through the gap in the ice, and I saw this little guy, he was trapped in an empty beer can. I actually had to go half in the lake, to save him, and I realised, he's not a turtle, he's a tortoise. I just knew I needed to keep him." Said Louis, holding up a miniature tortoise. "Oh! And I saw something called, a pigeon."

"Interesting, and Mr Locksmith, are you planning to get a tank for this little, 'guy'?" Sir Davie answered, in a very, phoney, posh accent.

"Yeah, oh yeah. I found a little tank lying around by the campsite, over there. I kind of stole it, but it was collecting dust so I assumed they didn't want it anymore." Louis replied anxiously.

Sir Davie smiled suspiciously at him, and then said, "Miss Carneego? What about you?"

"Well Sir, I happened to find a baby horse. It had been stuck, on a mountain ledge and, of course, I flew to it. It had nothing wrong with it so I didn't have to heal it. You may be wondering how I got it down? Well, in my spare time I have been reading, 'Movements and Actions of Wingcraft' and I have been practicing some of the actions on page four hundred and ninety two, and one just *happened* to be a net wing move. Along the way I also saw several birds. A Robin, I believe, a Crow, a murder of which, and a blackbird. I also spotted a beaver, a deer, and a hedgehog." Shannon bragged intimidatingly.

"Well, quite a lot to share haven't you? Where may he stay?" Sir Davie answered, sounding proud, yet unimpressed. He was pointing to the large white horse that stood behind Shannon.

"Well Sir, I knew that I would be asked that, so I 'texted' my friend Lucia, whose mother works for the WBAPO-" (The Winged Being Abuse Prevention Office,) "And asked her to ask her mother to talk to the committee, about making animal shelters for horses, dogs, cats, and many, many more. Lucia said she may get back to me tomorrow morning, and, until then, I may tie Snow to the front gates by a rope as we await the incoming builders." Shannon replied, bossily.

"Very well planned Miss Carneego, very well planned. Mr Barnumbio, what about you?" Sir Davie asked, too seriously for his personality.

"Well. I saved a pig. He was being hurt by people who wanted to cook him alive, at the campsite! I got him. He is a baby. I called him Piglet, since he is one. And I saw a seagull." Michael answered quickly, and shyly.

Sir Davie rubbed him on the back, and Luna saw him whisper something in his ear, that looked like, 'Well done. You're really getting better at handling your anxiety.' Luna smiled. Louder, Sir Davie said, "Now Miss Copper. What have you found? Then we may actually have to head home, I'd planned to go to two other places, but we were here for *far* too long." Sir Davie said, looking at his watch. "Oh! Yeah, it's quarter to nine. Jeezo, how did that happen?"

"I actually found four animals. They were together though. They're cats. One is ginger, one is white with one ginger *ear,* and two are white. Three of them were on the ice and one was unconscious under it. They are all healthy now, except the one who was under the ice is 'weak'." Luna replied, almost as quickly as Michael.

"Good. Where are they? And will they be kept in your dorm Miss Copper?" Asked Sir Davie.

"They're in my bag. And yes, they will be kept in my dorm Sir. Oh and, er, who is, er, checking if they are, you know, boys, or er, girls?" Luna answered nervously, and clueless.

"That's fine, and you will, unluckily, be the one who checks that. Although, luckily you don't need to do it the, well, usual way. I'm handing you all these little bowls. And when one drinks from one. In large, bold writing, it'll say, BOY, or, GIRL. Then, you will name them." And no, it doesn't work on humans Mr Lochsmith." Sir Davie answered, as Louis' hopeful hand, went down. Sir Davie handed them all a small white bowl each, and nodded.

Luna opened her bag, took out each cat, and fed them all water, fresh from her bowl. The ginger cat, was a boy. The older white one, was a girl. And the two kittens, were both boys.

"Sir Davie! I've done the tests. You can have this back!" Luna yelled, holding her bowl in the air. Sir Davie walked, rather seriously, to a small tree.

"Alright Miss Copper, I'll take that." he said, and he picked up the bowl, and put it in his pocket. "Now, you just have to name them, there are

Winglet collars in the staff room, but I can make them tighter, and they'll fit perfectly. You can write their new names onto the paper attached to the collars. 'Might as well take one for Glee too." He smiled, and produced a small yellow whistle from behind his shirt.

He blew it, but instead of whistling, it flew happily around, and tapped each student on the shoulder, which made them all look round. Then it flew back to Sir Davie, and reattached itself to the string. "Ok, well it is seven minutes until we are due at the school, so I'm afraid you are all going to have to pick some Starweed, and that will get us back *just* in time for the partnered dance." Sir Davie yelled.

Luna put the cats in her bag, and stumbled over to Louis. "What, *is,* Starweed? And, er, what does it, *do?*" She said, anxiously.

"It is the weed of speed. It is extremely, toxic to eat, but if you rub it around your wings, then apparently, it makes you faster." He replied, smartly. "It's, blue stemmed, it's got purple leaves, and occasionally star shaped, green, flowers. It only lasts for around five minutes though. Lucky for us, it only grows by water so there's heaps."

Luna tried hard, to nod, as if she understood. Although, she was confused at an unnatural level. Once Louis noticed, he pointed to a purple bush across the lake, then Luna had a better idea of what she was looking for.

"Please go pick it now. Then go in the direction of the campsite. You'll find yourselves at school again in around four minutes. Then change into your 'fancy' clothes and return to the hall for the dancing." Sir Davie explained, kindly.

Luna, Louis, Michael, and Shannon all headed for either the forest, the other side of the lake, or the campsite, where a small bush was stood behind a small green tent. As Luna arrived at the campsite, she wandered over to the bush. Suddenly the resident of the green tent emerged.

It was a small, blonde haired girl. Who had short, blonde hair and who looked only slightly older than Luna.

"Oh! Oh, it's only you. You gave me a fright! Who, are~" Luna was stopped, by the girl. Who grabbed her arm, and pulled her in the tent without a word.

CHAPTER SIX : JANNETE, APRIL, MAE, AND JUNE'S BIG LIE

Inside, there was a decent amount of space, and two other girls. All of which, looked *exactly* like the girl who had pulled Luna inside.

"Ha, ha. I, I get it. This is some sort of, sort of, club, isn't it? And you want, me to, join it? Well, I'm not interested, thanks for the offer though." Luna hurried, and she reached for the opening.

"I don't recommend that. It, isn't where you think." Said a girl, who was sitting on a purple cushion on the ground reading a book, titled, 'Plants and Places of Wingcraft'. "We have moved."

Luna laughed phonily. "Yeah, yeah ok, er, where are we, then? And, who are you guys?"

The girl who stood behind her sat down, the girl reading a book marked her page, and put the book on the ground. The other girl, who was mixing a black substance, threw her pestle and mortar in front of her. As Luna got creeped, they all stared at her.

Once a few moments had passed, the girl who had pulled her in, replied, "I'm Jannete. Spelt, jay, a, en, en, ee, tee, ee. Jannete Stooper. This is April." She pointed at the girl reading a book, "And this is Mae. We're identical quadruplets." She pointed at the girl with the pestle and mortar.

"But there's, only three of you." Luna replied, not thinking straight, "And are you, are you Mae Stooper? Coco told me about you."

"Well done. That's how names work, yes. I'm Mae Stooper. Ugh, are you talking about, about, about Coco, Coco *Wheezleberry*?" Mae replied, laughing, but frowing.

"Cool. And yes, I am. She's, my best friend. Why?" Luna replied.

"Well, her family has never liked us. Too jealous I reckon. We live in a mansion, whereas they, they live in a one room flat near London." replied April.

"Hey! She is *not!* She never told me she was jealous! And she's not! You liar! Tell me then, tell me. The *entire* story." Luna screamed angrily.

Jannete replied, "Fine. Well, it all started in the year, nineteen fourteen, when great great great granny Margaret lived, and Coco's great great great granny Elizabeth lived. They were best friends all through primary, and high school. Until it came to University. They stayed in all the same classes, and sat next to each other every time. Although Margaret moved. She moved to Hong Kong. Because her dad lived there and she wanted to be closer to him. Elizabeth, however, wanted to go too, although she got pregnant with Coco's great great grandpa John at seventeen. She had to stay in England, but what she had no idea about, was that Margaret had moved, not only to be with her dad, but to sell. She sold almost everything, except from a smashed photo of her and Elizabeth as two year olds. When Elizabeth found out that Margaret had earned over a million pounds from selling antiques and china dolls, she immediately tried to compete. She sold everything. Literally. It was rather suspicious that she sold it all to one single old man. Her money was in her pocket, and it was real. Two years afterwards, when her son was two, she realised she had sold boxes of stuff. One of the boxes had a letter from Margaret inside, which she had written her full address, and phone number onto. Elizabeth grabbed her son, some clothes, and her old high school graduation photo, and took the plane to Hong Kong to see if her friend was still alive. The plane crashed, seeing as it wasn't as good quality back then, and Elizabeth passed away, although John survived, and grew up in a 'foster home'. The same foster home as Margaret's daughter Charlie. Because they both died, Margaret of murder, and Elizabeth in a plane crash, the Wheezleberry's are jealous, because we kept half a million pounds and earned more, whereas whenever a Wheezleberry is born, the police need to know who the parents are, and need to keep an eye on the parents, and the child, because they suspect Elizabeth sold the letter purposefully, which she probably did, and suspect that she wanted her old best friend to die because she had became rich in only days, and Elizabeth had gotten half as much and spent it all to look after her son. I am not saying she was right though she probably tried to get her murdered. In my opinion."

Luna's face rushed bright red. "It was clearly an accident! And even if it wasn't! Coco is in a whole other generation. Elizabeth and Margaret were in the nineteens! She's nothing like her! And she'll never be!" She felt her small part of vast cruelty begin to rise up through her stomach.

Jannete, April, and Mae all kept kindly, calm faces. April replied, "Well, I guess a friend of one would think that, it's an opinion Jan, just an opinion. We, however, need to remember that we study more than others, we know otherwise."

Luna's face could have popped with fury, "How dare you! I have a friend, who is one of the few people who like me, then all of a sudden, I'm wrong about what sort of person she is! Really! At least I don't have a friend who goes around putting people in the hospital! At least I have someone! Someone my species!" She hadn't thought of the words that had just flew from between her lips.

The girls looked as though they could cry. Mae finally raised her voice, "How dare you! You have no idea how hard we are working to save June! We would trade our *lives*, for hers! How do you even know about that anyways! She's only struck once! And it's because that stupid boy kept worrying about it too much!"

Luna was breathing heavily, before she spoke, she saw Jannete mouth to her, "Sorry, we'll sort her out, stay the night if you want to, we'll get back to the school at around eleven thirty tomorrow morning." Luna let a fake smile slip, then began arguing more, "Well that, 'stupid boy' was my friend Louis! I had to cure him! All because you couldn't help your identical twin quadruplet!" Mae looked angrily at her. Then picked up a small robot with wings, and it pushed Luna out onto the wet ground below, then it locked the opening, and zoomed through the top window into the tent.

Luna stared at her scraped knee, then looked around, she was, as the girls had explained, in a completely separate location. She appeared to be sitting in a puddle, with her bag on, and her yellow jumpsuit going an orange colour, she heard the faint meowing of a kitten, which made her stand up, open her bag up, and pick out the only awake kitten, it was the white one, which had one ginger ear. It purred softly into her hair. Luna looked round and noticed the time, it was half past nine, exactly.

"Ugh!" She thought, as she remembered the dance. She put her bag back on, and held the kitten closely in her arms. As she blew her hair out of her face, she saw the tent shrink perfectly to the size of a nearby drainpipe, of which it slid into and out of sight. Luna looked around curiously. She noticed it was very dark, although it was midnight, but she most definitely knew it wasn't. Around her, was what looked like an abandoned little city, of which she didn't know if she was near the school or not. Although the city had a strange, unstable feeling about it. It had vines and dead flowers which had took over, and the windows of the buildings seemed to be mostly smashed. Although there was a large hill, which a large castle stood upon.

She realised that she was standing on the road, so she immediately ran to a grass patch near a park. She sat unhappily on a swaying swing, and took out her book of animals. As she read a lot of facts about the 'Red Squirrel', she was accompanied by her pet Winglet, Glee, who had a piece of paper rolled around his wing.

She unwrapped the blue ribbon around it, and noticed it was a letter! Signed off by Rogererare. It read;

Dearest Miss Copper,

Us teaching staff would just like to ask you if you arrived safely, we asked Miss Stooper and her sisters to drop you off, as you probably know. Now I'm unfortunately not sure where exactly you are, but if you find the Wing shop - it's disguised as a, what they call, phone shop, but for the gifted it is a wing shop. Once you find it, I would like you to go towards the red building. It should have wooden doors. Then go around the desk, and down the ladder to the stone room, where you should meet your four friends, who have something they would like to share with you. I believe it is both a mixture of good news, and bad news. They also asked me to ask you to be there by nine fifty seven.

Please return soon,

Your headmaster, Rogererare

Luna re-wrapped the ribbon around the paper, then put the kitten back in the bag. She looked around mischievously, and not long after that saw the phone company logo, it happened to be a circle with two horizontal lines in the middle, displayed on a large white building with white, wooden doors.

She flew to it, and stared blankly around. There was no sign of any red building. She looked at the note, and convinced herself that it was meant to be, a *red building.* As she stared, an outline of a large building began to take form by the park. As it grew clearer and clearer, Luna realised the colour of it was a dark shade of red. Alike the blood that drew from her elbow just over a month beforehand.

She noticed a beaded door next to a window (lined with rot and, what Luna thought to be old doughnuts.)

She took her wings off, and hid them in her jumpsuit pocket, then ran across the road and through the door. As she walked in, she realised the desk was wrecked too. It seemed to have been graffitied, with unpleasant words that made Luna feel shook. She walked around it, careful not to touch anything, and saw Coco with her head popped out of a hole in the ground. Luna couldn't believe her eyes.

"Oh! Hi! You will never believe this! Well, some of it, some of it is good, some is quite horrific. But anyways! Come, come! Louis, Skye, and Anna are down there too. We got dressed by the way, and the dance, well, you'll find out soon. Come!" Coco said excitingly.

"Ok, ok! But, tell me the bad news first." Luna replied, exasperated. And she climbed down the ladder, Coco below her.

When she got to the bottom, Coco whispered in everyone's ear, except Luna's.

Louis suddenly said, "Ok, I need to tell you the bad news, then Coco will tell you the good news." Everyone nodded. "Well there's two pieces of bad news. Number one is, well, we found out that, well, sorry we found this out, but, er, well, your mum died in the plane crash, but your dad, he, he er, well, he committed a, a crime, and he went to prison for it. He, *really* wanted to be there for you. But he, he started doing serial crimes, I'm sorry." He looked nervous.

Luna stopped, she froze, and then she felt her face get very wet with tears. "What else, just don't mention that again, please?" She said, as she wiped her eyes with her hands.

"Ok, we won't. But there's only one worse thing. Well, we saw, well, we saw June, she is the first Comporatora to ever walk on earth. And that, really, is not good. And-" Coco nudged him.

"On a lighter note, the dance ended early because of seventh years being stupid. But I have a piece of incredible news! Ryan, my big brother, works for a house decoration company, thing. Right." Coco interrupted. Luna nodded, "Well he has given me paints, flooring, mops, cleaning stuff, window cleaners, enchanting hider juice, doors, nails and screws, a toolbox, wallpaper, and he paid for this place. He gave me this 'guide' for help, and he said that we can make ourselves a clubhouse! And, we can stay here in the holidays too! Because Louis, in the summer is allowed to come for sleepovers or flying games or anything if he tells James. Anna is the same, Skye's parents go on holidays to Mexico each holiday, and she usually needs to stay with her auntie, but unfortunately she died, and I, well, I can, and your grandparents probably won't mind. So, we get to completely transform this place. And! There's exactly seven rooms! So we can have a kitchen and stuff, and like maybe a hangout or something, in one room, and we can have a bathroom, in one room, and, we can each have like a, bedroom or something. I dunno. Just. We have a clubhouse! Ryan gave it to us! And Anna loves baking, so she is going to make new doughnuts and cakes for the window! It's just going to be amazing! Said Coco, jumping excitedly.

"Cool! At least I don't need to go back to my grandparent's hou~" Luna stopped. She remembered something, something important, very important. She knew the only way to save this memory was to go to a place of which she knew she was not welcome. "I, I'm sorry, I need, I need to go." she said.

"Wait why?" Coco yelled. Luna ran outside, put her wings on, and flew to 74 Moonlight Avenue. She walked inside the house, and sat on the stairs, waiting.

CHAPTER SEVEN : ROGERERARE

A few hours later, the Silverhood's returned from their Friday night restaurant dinner, and when they did, they weren't happy that Luna was waiting for them.

"What are you doing here? You don't belong here. What am I supposed to do with you?" said, Luna's grandfather.

"I ask one thing, can I, please, get my box, that's all I want." Luna begged, "Please! I need it." Luna's grandmother, Molly, took a breath, cleared her throat, and stared at Luna as if she were some kind of burglar.

"Who do you think you are? You know you are not welcome. This is our last day with Alexandra, and you need to come barging in like an angry rhino. What a disgraceful young girl you are, just like your parents. You can go upstairs. Go get whatever items from your room as you want, and *never* return. Do you understand? You have quarter of an hour, oh and take that wretched bear you have. I can never stand it!" She said, "Oh Alexandra, no worries baby girl, that horrible beast of a girl is leaving us." She yelled into the kitchen.

"Coming Granny!" Luna heard Alex shout, from the kitchen. As she arrived in the hall, she passed Luna a folded piece of paper when her grandparents were looking in the living room. Luna smiled, and glanced at the paper;

Luna, I'll write to you as much as I can, here's my new address, 55 Honty Street. Just write back when you can. I'll miss you. Bye **xxxxx**

Alex nodded, and Luna smiled. She put the paper in her pocket, and ran upstairs. She grabbed the old, rusty, box, that her dad had used to carry her mums wedding ring inside, and she ran for the window, only, it was locked, and the door was too! "No! No!" She yelled.

Her grandmother laughed behind the door, "Haha! You will stay in there until further notice. There should be a couple of carrot sticks on the windowsill if you want some. But just stay in there." she said.

"Why!" Luna asked, "Because you don't like me? Well, that's not my problem!"

Luna's grandmother replied, "No! Because, I hated your father, such a goodie goodie, I don't want another one in the family. Now goodnight!"

Luna slammed herself on her mattress, until she felt a faint vibration on her side. She curled her wing up and realised she had received a long message.

Coco wheezleberry went online

[Coco Wheezleberry] Luna? Are you ok? Don't worry about the clubhouse, I wasn't a fan very much, I just thought it was something you would like. So I sold it to an elderly man, who didn't have a decent home, but his daughter paid me 1000 pounds! Oh my gosh!

Luna copper went online

[Luna Copper] I'm fine thanks, it's just, I had this, weird thought. And that's great! You keep the money though, your family needs it.

[Coco Wheezleberry] Yes I know! I will, what do you mean? Sudden thought?

[Luna Copper] I dunno. Well, I just, I have this, this jewellery box. And my dad held my mums wedding ring in

it. I just, sometimes I need it, to put my worries and things in it. Sorry if I sound like a baby, I just, wish they were here : (

[Coco Wheezleberry] No! You're not a baby! My parents are a right pain in the backside, but I can't imagine a life without them, I have no idea how it must feel. If its upsetting you? You could go to the worry lab? It's down near London, but we could fly there easily, it only costs you fifteen pounds. They basically jag you, and make a juice for you. If you drink it, after 24 hours the worry goes away, I did it once. Any other thoughts?

[Luna Copper] Nah, thanks for the offer, but I don't think I need it. Yes actually, you said something about June Stooper?

[Coco Wheezleberry] Oh yeah! Well, she somehow is the only Comporatora in history, to actually be real, and walk on earth! Unfortunately, the tracks she made are only 102 feet away from the school! All students have been asked to stay inside until further notice, dunno what's happening? Oh, and by the way, where are you? Rogererare asked me if I knew where you were, he wants you in his office as soon as possible.

[Luna Copper] Oh! That's bad! And, I'm trapped in my room at the BH, bad house really. HELP ME!

[Coco Wheezleberry] Er, I cant. Try the window.

[Luna Copper] Oh, wish I had thought of that!

[Coco Wheezleberry] Just smash it then, Rogererare really wants you!

[Luna Copper] Isn't that mean though?

[Coco Wheezleberry] LUNA!

[Luna Copper] Ugh fine! See you in a bit.

[Coco Wheezleberry] See you.

Luna copper went offline

Coco wheezleberry went offline

Luna grabbed her bag of kittens, and stood by the window. She watched it thoughtfully for a while, then took a breath, and punched it. The glass shattered all over the floor, and Luna's grandfather started stomping upstairs. As he began unlocking the door. Luna picked up her box, and jumped out the window. As she rose up towards the hill, she saw the faint outline of a creature take form by the school, but it then arose to her height. She stopped, so did the creature.

After she had begun flying backwards, the creature came with speed towards her. As it became clearer, she could see the two uneven, sized wings, the empty eye socket, the long snout, and the tail, of the one and only, June, Stooper.

Luna screamed, and June stopped in front of her. She put her paw on Lunas head.

"Look, I don't want to give you any disrespect, but I'm absolutely terrified of you!" Luna yelled, looking June straight in the eye. June roared angrily, and Luna began falling, her wings wouldn't flap! June stared at her as she fell. Before hitting the ground and collapsing, Luna saw a bright red light, form in a ball around June, and a haul of students pour out from the school.

Luna had awoken in a pitch black room, which seemed to go on forever. She walked and walked until she walked into a window. Outside, was a ceiling, a ceiling of which looked like a dormitory. It was as if she had been seeing through the sight of a wakening student. A few seconds later, Luna recalled a horrible thought. But no, it couldn't be, someone would know, someone would have to. It wouldn't make sense.

As if on cue, three of the Stooper quadruplets rushed into sight, one shouting, one crying, and the other trying to see the positive, but once the bushy wall of golden hair covered the screen, Luna knew that she was seeing through either, June, Mae, April, or Janet's vision, although, it could only be one of the four, only one was a resident of the school, so that meant, she was seeing Mae Stooper's eyesight.

As she tried to smash the glass, it only appeared back instantly. Luna had another random thought, she could just text Coco, yeah, that's what she'll do! As she reached for her phone, she was surprised to see that it was working! She texted Coco immediately;

Luna copper went online

[Luna Copper] COCO! HELP! EMERGENCY! I'M TRAPPED IN MAE'S MIND! HELP!

It delivered, but Coco only replied when Luna had watched Mae get washed, do her hair, get dressed, and open a letter from her grandmother.

Coco wheezleberry went online

[Coco Wheezleberry] Don't worry, me and Louis are on our way, just, hang in there, if our antidote doesn't work, then there's only two options, we kill Mae, or we wait for her to suffer and die, we stole this from Mrs Penny's cupboard!

[Luna Copper] OK OK! JUST, GET ME OUT!

[Coco Wheezleberry] Hey! We are just heading up the girl's staircase, we'll be there in one minute, just keep watching!

[Luna Copper] Ok! Just, hurry!

Coco wheezleberry went offline

Luna copper went offline

A couple of minutes later, Coco, and Louis, arrived in the dormitory. The quadruplets screamed in fright, but Louis explained why they were there, and Louis sat on the bed Mae was sitting on, and said, "Look, take this medicine, swallow it, and stay still, this might hurt your eyes for a minute, but that's because we are summoning Luna from your brain." Mae screamed again.

"Ugh come on Stooper!" Coco said impatiently, "It's not that bad, well, it's either that, or you both DIE!" Louis gave her a disgusted look, and she looked away.

Louis handed Mae a cup of green substance, and she simply stared at it.

"Drink it. Please? I almost died from your sister but I'm trying to save my best friend and you from dying too. Please, drink it." Louis said calmly.

"I... I... Cant! I just can't!" Mae yelled, and she stood up. Luna was fuming at her. Why not! She mumbled.

Louis looked at her, "Why! Please! Then it will all end. Please!" he said.

Luna felt a vein pop right out of her head in fury. Mae started crying, "I... I... Don't want to!"

~"Why! Not!"~

~"Because! I!"~

~"Just do it!"~

~"I can't!"~

~"Why not! You foolish brat! Just do it! Save yourself!"~

~"I can't! Because! I should have been the one who saved this! I should!"~

~"You absolute brat! You won't save two lives because you're jealous! You're jealous! That you can't be the hero every second of every day! You foolish, foolish, brat!"~

Coco pushed Louis out of the way and said, "Look! If you don't drink this tiny cup of medicine! Then I will kill, you! Just take it and then carry on being the spoiled girl you are!" Luna's nostrils were flaring, her eyes were so thin that she looked like a cat, her face was bright red. She let out a roar of anger. Just afterwards, Mae screamed, "Fine!" at Coco, and swallowed the medicine. Luna felt queasy, she felt dizzy. Her head hurt, and she began to float peacefully in mid-air. Then she appeared to be spinning, so quickly indeed, that she felt as if she was about to vomit, then she stood wobbling in front of her two friends. Then her stomach did a chortle, and she fell backwards into Louis's arms. He laughed, and Coco smiled, Luna blinked and fell asleep, mid blink!

Meanwhile, Coco and Louis did a silent high five, and the quadruplets comforted Mae, as she vomited right over her bed.

Whispering, Louis said to Coco, "I think we should put her in bed, she was unconscious all night so most likely she doesn't remember sleeping." Coco nodded, and they walked to Luna's dormitory, dorm 865, and laid her in bed.

Once Luna had started snoring, Louis and Coco went to find Rogererare, to inform him that Luna would see him in an hour or two. As they arrived in his office, he was at the open window, with a green, large, winglet, on the windowsill, he was tying a letter onto its wing, and he let it fly professionally away. He turned around to look at them.

"Well, hello, may I help you two?" He said.

"Yes Sir, just to let you know that Luna will be here to talk to you in around two hours." Louis answered.

"Ah yes, any time before one would be great, thank you. I hope you got your homework folders for this term, the Valentines Break is coming in two weeks, and we still haven't received all of the nineteen one essays, it will be a large part in your exams next term." Rogererare replied.

"Er, no Sir." Coco replied anxiously. Louis gave her a nudge and winked at her. She nodded.

"Well then, I'd better be off. I need to go to a short staff meeting, I am expecting Miss Copper here when I get back." Rogererare said, and he stood up, rustled his papers, and opened the door for them to exit. They walked out the door, and went to the south hall, otherwise known as, the chatting hall, because it was always very full with chatter, that you were very unlikely to be overheard if you wanted to chat.

They found a table, and sat down, once a few silent minutes had passed, Louis asked, "Well, what do you have planned for over the break?"

Coco thought for a minute, then replied, "Oh, well, probably just hang around the den, with Amber, Ryan and Rachel and stuff, you know."

"Oh, cool, where's your den?" Louis asked, intrigued.

"Well, it's under the tree near 'Snacky Macky Pizza Place', it's cool. I share it with Ryan, Rachel, and Amber." Coco answered.

Louis nodded coolly, "D'you go there a lot?"

Coco laughed, "Yeah! I practically l- wait! Why do you want to know? Who told you? Whatever it is! Its not true!" She picked up her book, and ran out of the hall. Louis called after her, but she had already sprinted up to the 'girls' dormitories. He looked worryingly at the door, until he saw Luna run through the crowds of pupils and sit beside him.

"Oh, er, hi!" He said, but he was still looking at the door.

"Hi. What is it? What's wrong?" Luna asked worryingly, she looked at the door, and back at Louis.

"Well." Replied Louis, turning round and pulling the mac, n, cheese bowl towards him, "It was just, Coco. She, she was telling me about her 'den' and when I asked her if she goes there often she just ran away."

Luna looked confused, "Hmm, that is weird. Did she tell you what it was like?"

"Well, not really. She just told me she shared it with Ryan, Rachel, and Amber." Louis answered, truthfully.

"Where did she go? I'll go talk to her." Luna responded.

"To the girl's dorms, I would come, but I'm not allowed, I think I broke the rules when we broke the Comporarora chain. Sorry." Louis answered guiltily. "When you're gone I'll start on our nineteen one essay. I have the book."

Luna nodded, and ran to the staircase, as Louis picked up a quill. She knocked on Coco's dormitory door, but there was no answer, she knocked again, and Coco just told her to go away.

"Come on, you can tell me. I'm your friend, that's what I am for. Let me in." Luna said. Coco snuffled, and opened the door, wiping her eyes.

"I'm not the important thing. Well, not now anyways. *sniff* you should probably, *sniff* go see Rogererare. He really, really, *sniff* wanted you. Then we can talk if *sniff* you really want, after." She said miserably, Luna raised her eyebrows.

"Well, ok. But we will talk. Swear?" Luna replied.

"Swear!" Coco replied depressingly, and she shut the door. Luna continued up the stairs, and went along the East corridor on the fourth floor, until she approached Rogererare's office, knocked four times and entered when he said so.

"Why hello. I only just got back too! May you take a seat? I have a few things to talk to you about." He said, motioning Luna to the chair opposite him.

She sat down and looked at him. "Yes Sir?"

"Well, I have two suggestions and one favour. Well, I know there is a bit of, mystery, for you and your friends, so have you ever thought about talking to them about everything you know already and seeing how they might link up?" He asked.

"Actually we haven't, no, but I certainly will ask them Sir." Luna replied.

"Very good, very good. And, we are taking four females, and four males from first year. To see if they would like to take more Winghinging classes and try out for the First Year Eagles team. We've got our Ravens. You'll play for the rest of your years at Winged Beauties. The Raven Finder is Ruby Carneego, Hitters are Jack Madfore, and John Sweatheart. And the Goaler is Jasmine Mundelio. We would like you to try out as Finder, the two hitter female competitors are Bonnie Charl and Hannah Anderson. And the Goaler female is Skye Macdonaldson. The male Finder is Justin Miller, the male Hitters are Louis Lochsmith and Charlie White, and the Goaler is Andrew Ubby. Does this seem like something you would like to try out?" He asked.

"Well, ok. But, would I be playing against Jasmine?" Luna asked feverishly.

"Yes, whenever you had a match. The pitch is ten kilometres south of the school. You would train with your team every Monday and every Thursday." He replied.

"Ok, you said you had a favour?" Luna asked.

"Yes, may I borrow Glee? To send a letter, my Winglet, Sharnade, she's sending a letter and she's late back." Rogererare asked hopefully.

"Er, sure? Just make sure he comes back ok." Luna replied. "Anything else?"

"No no, Professor Fire will meet you in his office tonight. Any plans tomorrow Miss Copper?" Rogererare replied.

Luna was wondering why her headmaster was asking her if she was doing anything on a Sunday, and if it was worth telling him about where she was going at midnight, but she decided to just reply, "Er, no. No, I'm free tomorrow."

Rogererare smiled, "Why that's good. Well, better be off then shouldn't you? Remember, put the clues together and find the solution. Good day." He motioned Luna to the door and she walked down the stairs to where Louis was still writing the essay, his ink bottle finished.

Luna sat opposite him and said, "Take a break, what page are you on now? Ten?"

"Eleven, actually. What did RR want?" Louis replied, as he placed his quill down.

Excuse me? Does 'RR' stand for Rogererare?" Luna asked.

"Yes, but what did he want?" Louis replied, his eyes wide.

"Well, he er, told me to get you and Coco, maybe Skye and Anna but I'm not sure, and see if anything connects up with all of the weird things that have been happening, and, oh he asked me to try out for the First Year Eagles Team, I think I'll do it." She replied.

"Cool, he asked Skye as well though, I think. Well, I guess we'll find out tonight. What place are you supposed to be in? I'm only Hitter, nothing much." He held his hand in an awkward position, "Shame though, Ruby

Carneego as Finder? Jack Madfore and John Sweatheart as Hitters? And to top it all off, Jasmine Mundelio as Goaler! The Ravens will be pretty difficult to beat."

"Nah, Hitter is good, I'm Finder, well, hopefully." Luna replied.

"Cool, anyways, I, got to... Go, yeah, got to, never mind. Bye, see you at try outs." he replied.

Luna nodded, and said. "Ok, see you, I've got to go see Coco anyway, bye." Louis left the room, and Luna read through her, Louis' and Coco's nineteen one essay, and noticed that he had only put his name on the paper, she used the remaining drop of ink on the quill to scribble, '+ Luna + Coco', neatly on the line, and then ran upstairs to talk to Coco about what was bothering her.

"Hi." she said, as she wandered into the dorm, Coco waved and smiled phonily at her. "What happened today? We only have nine hours before we need to go down to the basement, so I want to know what is wrong and why your upset. You know you can tell me anything. That's what I exist for."

Coco remained silent, but patted her bed next to her. Luna sat down. There was a moment where Coco had inhaled and not exhaled, but once she did, she said, "I, I didn't want to say, because I wanted us to all be friends still, but once I found out Louis was the same as well, I, I thought it would help." Luna gave her a look of 'go-on', "Well, you see, 'the den' is, it's where me, Rachel, Ryan and Amber live. Our parents, I don't know, and our other siblings, not sure either, but, er, I'm an, an, an orphan too, I, I think. Sorry." She started crying again.

"Oh, oh, I, oh." Luna replied, "Can I get Louis, Anna, and Skye?" Coco nodded, her head still in her hands. Luna patted her on the shoulders and ran to where Skye and Anna were sitting at a table in the main hall, Skye waved and pulled out a chair, then continued chatting.

"-It was so adorable!" Anna finished, as she welcomed Luna to the table. Skye giggled squeakily, then she hi'd at Luna.

Before Luna had gotten the chance to talk, Skye put her head on her fist and fluttered her long, long eyelashes, "So, what's Louis writing? A cry for help? A love letter? A letter to RR about getting us more homework?" She said.

"Er, are you guys the Skye and Anna I know? Why do you all of a sudden have some sort of attitude with Louis?" Luna asked coldly.

"He was extremely rude to us, he, he, he called us, us, chatterboxes!" Skye and Anna said sympathetically, "Be quiet, I can hear you from over here you chatterboxes! Ugh! How mean!" Anna added mockingly.

"Well, you know what, I don't have time for this nonsense, anyway, I don't know what he's writing? But you might want to go see Coco, she has some interesting news, anyway, I'll go talk to him." Luna replied. She pointed at Louis, who's nose was buried in a piece of paper, his hand gripped tightly around a quill. Skye and Anna looked at her in confusion.

"You'll see." she replied. They shrugged, and ran out of the hall. Luna stood up and walked over to Louis.

"Hi Louis. What're you writing?" Luna said, trying with much difficulty, to act casual.

Louis flushed and tucked the paper under the table, "Umm, just, just, you know, extra homework, I guess, yes. Just homework, that's all." Luna could tell that Louis was struggling just as much as she was to act casual.

She remembered how angry the girls were, so, to stop something horrible, she decided to say, "Oh, can I have a look? I need some more information for some of the exams." Louis blushed and blinked, he swore he needed the bathroom immediately and picked up the paper as he rushed through the crowd of students, a few spare sheets fell to the ground.

CHAPTER EIGHT: LOUIS LETTERS, AND MIDNIGHT MURDERING

Louis had been gone for almost ten minutes now, and Luna had gotten bored. She picked up a piece of paper from the ground and took a quill out of her bag. As she looked around, she noticed the Chubby twins, (Shubber twins), open her other bag and began throwing the cats to one another, Luna had blankly forgotten about the kittens and once realising, reacted instantly.

"Hey! Hey leave them alone! Chad! Parker! Put. The. Kittens. Down. Now!" She said angrily. She sprinted over to them and removed the cats physically from their grasp.

"Ooh! Is little orphan Luna looking after wittle baby kitties. How cute!" Parker mimicked stupidly.

"Ah shut up!" Luna yelled and she walked away as they sniggered. She sat back down and turned over the paper, ready to begin sketching, although what she found was not a blank sheet. No, it was;

Dear Master,

Yes. I am ready. The girl is all set up. Where did you get that RR mask from? It must have worked, she is definitely coming tonight.

The others, where are they? They should be here by now. Or shall I meet them in the basement at twelve am? Is Collin coming? He is your best commander, he could help a lot, and I'm here too though of course.

Who else do you want me to trap? How many? I can get that, Alexandra girl Luna was talking about?

Yours sincerely,

Louis Lochsmith

Luna coughed. The cats hissed. The hall went dangerously silent. And yet, her head was not moving from the letter. She managed to twist her head to the side, although what she saw, as heart wrenching as it was, it revealed so many answers. A young, burnt to crisp, violet eyed, version of Louis. She tried to scream but it only blocked her breath, he was holding her by the neck, she couldn't breathe, she was yelling, then, total blackness. Nothing.

She awoke with a cackle. A few gunshots, and a cackle.

"Good morning Luna, how did you sleep?" Said a rotten, nasty, old voice.

"Not so good actually." Luna replied, awkwardly casually.

"Um, ok." Said the voice. "I have four of your mates. Let's play a game. If you give me the answers to these four questions, you can get two of them, and my secret. Am I clear?" Luna sighed. "AM I CLEAR!"

"Fine! Your clear you stupid, stupid, thing!" Luna yelled back, "Tell me the questions!" Coco gave a shriek of terror and then closed her mouth as the coal man sharpened his wings.

"Well, firstly, how did you escape that Comporatora trap?" He replied coldly.

"Well, firstly," Luna mimicked. "You knew about that? You set that up? And to let you know, I had something, something none other Comporatora victims had. A mobile."

"STOP LYING!" He shrieked.

A soothing voice sounded, the same voice from Luna's dream, it said, "She is telling the truth Barney."

"Ok brother. Calm down." Barney sounded scared as he replied. Alex ran to Luna, who comforted her deeply. "Secondly, did you show our letter to any other little rodents?"

"No, no I didn't, but, I have a few questions myself actually, if, that's alright with you." Luna continued before even getting an answer. "For the voice actually. Who are you, and, who wrote that letter and if it was you, how have you been, 'watching' me?"

A few moments passed, and then the voice sounded once more, "Well, to answer your first question, I am your father, well, his soul. To answer your second, I wrote your letter, and, I've flew by your side your entire life sweetheart, your entire life, I always will, until you see me again, on the other side of life, I will never stop being by your side. I love you Luna."

Luna felt stupid, crying, for her dad, but she simply couldn't help it. "Ok, I, I miss you." She replied. She felt a soft pat on the back but Alex was standing farther away. She knew what it was.

"Right, I know I know, all lovey dovey but back to business. Question three, what was in that medicine you used to save the young boy in your hospital wing." He spat.

"Umm, no idea." She replied.

"Tell the truth and no one gets hurt."

"I don't know though."

"I repeat, tell the truth."

"I am!"

"TELL ME THE TRUTH!"

"I AM TELLING THE TRUTH!"

"Right. Last chance. Tell. Me. The. Truth."

"I. DON'T. KNOW. OR. CARE."

"Raise your guns and shoot." He told the coal men who held a strangled Coco.

"Wait." Luna said calmly as the man nodded. "Don't shoot." She looked at Coco and bowed her head. "Just. Don't shoot." She used a random wing movement to push Alex aside, and repeated, "Don't shoot. Please."

"Why shouldn't I?" Barney said coldly.

Luna took a shaky breath and answered, "Because to take someone's life because one didn't know all the answers is, it's something you would only do if there was point. What is the point?"

There was a minute or so of no noise, if you exclude Coco's struggling. Then Barney yelled, "SHOOT!"

"NO!" Luna yelped once more! "NO! NO!"

"RIGHT! Then give me the answer!" Before Barney continued, random words were yelled.

"Luba! Iv ge iz yoir hads grothed! Yen ge is hour ooncle!" There was no response.

"WHAT I WAS SAYING WAS GIVE ME THE ANSWER OR SHE DIES!"

"WHY, do you need the answer."

"Because, because I need to save~"

"Me. He needs to save me." Said the voice of Luna's father.

"But, but, how?" Luna felt a bit of embarrassment.

"We are brothers, darling, we are brothers. My soul lies here, but my body, organs, bones, blood, lies in Marig Hospital For Winged Injuries, your mothers however, no, not even a soul survived, hit and cracked in the brain, never good." Said Luna's father gently.

"But I thought you were barged into with *somebody's* military plane." Luna looked at Barney, who smirked.

"Yes, but that wasn't what killed me. Or, put me asleep."

"What!"

"A comporatora attack. I'm in Barneys' head."

"Wait, but why don't you just kill him then?"

"It's not that simple. His brain is different, I need him to save me so that I can be with you. But before he saves me he needs to have a certain amount of supporters, coal men. He has enough now but needs to make the medicine. He isn't actually bad, he is possessed, by the real, Barney Bubwul."

"But he is Barney Bubwul, isn't he?"

"No honey, no."

"Oh, well, wait, that means that Louis is his supporter? Can he, you know, escape?"

"Unfortunately, not. Unless you can kill the real Barney Bubwul, then no."

"Oh. But how do I kill him?" Luna asked casually. She looked at Barney once there was no answer and continued, "And can you *please* let her go? What did she do to you to deserve that?" Barney scowled then yelled at the coal man to release Coco, who ran into Luna and panted.

"Louis is cursed!" She yelled, oblivious to the fact that Luna had found that out hours beforehand.

"I know, I am standing literally right here." Luna replied savagely.

Barney slouched, Luna knew why, he was angry that he couldn't kill another person.

"I suppose, I can let you pass, on one condition. May you be happy if I let you go?" He said in a rather hopeful, yet low and angry voice.

Before Coco or Luna could reply, Alex decided she wanted to be part of the argument, "Yes! Let us go! You-" She was cut off by her own scream of agony, suddenly she had been punched unconscious by a rock solid piece of poison ivy, which Barney had summoned to her.

"HOW DARE YOU! YOU MONSTER! SHE WAS ONLY SAYING THAT SHE WANTED TO GET OUT!" Coco yelled in astonishment.

"Ugh shut up Wheezleberry, or you'll be next." Threatened Barney, which made Coco fall silent.

Luna looked into the violent eyes of the horrid, dangerous man, and saw what made her own eyes die.

He wasn't bad, not at all, he had the shadow of a young man screaming for life in his eyes, he was trapped, trapped inside the body of a criminal, no way to escape, just trapped in an eye. As she looked closer, something even more shocking met her eyes Barney was crying, but the tears were on the inside, his face was as dry and stubborn as it usually was, but he wasn't happy, not at all.

Without thinking, she walked slowly towards him and placed her hand on his shoulder.

"Luna! NO!" Coco yelled. Luna took no notice of this.

Barney looked bewildered, embarrassed, hypnotised, and angry, all at once.

Then he straightened up again, "How dare you touch me. How dare you."
He grabbed Luna by the collar of her top and resumed, "Oh ho, Copper you
have no idea what you have gotten yourself into. Absolutely no, idea."

Luna cried out, "What!" Then the forgotten voice of her father yelled
deafeningly, "IF YOU DARE TOUCH THAT LITTLE GIRL THEN MR
BUBWUL, YOU WILL REGRET THIS FOR THE REST OF YOUR
NEVERENDING LIFE!"

Barney let go and Luna fell to the floor with a clank, she had clearly
broken another bone, she couldn't tell if it was her shoulder blade or her
neck, but either way, she couldn't lift her head.

"Mr Lochsmith, I am too weak, she has figured out our secret. You take
over." Barney said weakly, then like that, he vanished.

Louis stood over the frozen Luna and stared at her, his violet eyes gleaming
with the light of the lightning, now shooting across the sky outside.

"Louis, please. Don't you remember? I'm your friend. Please, help me." Luna
begged.

"Mr Lochsmith does not have friends, his master controls him now, I may not
obey orders from the enemy, I must complete what we have started." he
answered in a robot like fashion. Then his eyes glowed, brighter than the
lightning, brighter than the sun, brighter then any light in the universe.
Then once again, the blackness of death or unconsciousness flew over Luna.
Then, it was all over.

CHAPTER NINE : NIGHTMARE AT WINGED BEAUTIES

Luna awoke to a deafening squeal, a familiar squeal. She spotted the cards and gifts and sweets at the end of her hospital bed but didn't bother a fudge cube. Who screamed, and why did it sound familiar? Luna stepped out of bed and ran through the velvet curtains around her.

Through the minuscule gap at the doors, she saw Coco, drenched in blood, and teachers running towards her, but of course, before she could sprint out the doors, Mrs Penny pulled her to her bed once more.

"WHAT DO YOU THINK YOU ARE DOING OUT OF BED WITH SUCH AN INJURY!" She yelled, it was only then when Luna realised she was wearing a rather large neck brace. She grunted with both anger and sadness. Then she sat on her bed and laid down.

A few moments had passed of Luna just looking at her presents, tempted to open them. Once she realised that Coco would most likely be joining her shorty, Luna decided to open a few.

From Coco, she received a small box of chocolates and a new timetable quill, (she knew it was for her timetable because of where it was bought, 'Tyler Taphops Shop for School Properties'. From Ruby, she received a card, and some flowers, pink and puffy. From Jasmine, a poison ivy sample with a label noting, 'Must Eat!' Luna just shrugged and chucked the ivy on the floor. The last present was a vast packet of lemon and strawberry sherbets. The note said from Skye and Anna.

Luna wanted to save the other lemon and strawberry sherbets for later, and she didn't want to open any more presents either, but as she tried to go to sleep, another scream shouted, but not recognisable, Luna tried going to the door but then stumbled backwards, Mrs Penny wasn't there though. She felt dizzy, sick, then her eyesight started going, she fell to the floor, yelped, and Mrs Penny jogged instantly towards her.

"Mrs Penny! Yes! Wait, no. No. No! Who screamed?" Luna mumbled as she grabbed Mrs Penny's shoulder so she could stand up.

"No one did darling. No one screamed. Are you dreaming?" Mrs Penny said worryingly. She started breathing heavily and all colour in her face drained away.

"No! I was *not* dreaming! I was wide awake! Someone screamed, ow! Out there! Like Coco did!" Luna yelled, Mrs Penny must have misunderstood. There was no way of not hearing that scream. No way.

"Perhaps you should lie down honey. Lie down, you're red, like, bright red. Oh my! I need to take your **temperature!**" As she said the last word, a flying thermometer flew into her hands, she pushed it to Lunas dry forehead, and gasped, "Oh my! 271c°! That's! That is outrageous!" Luna felt her forehead, and surely enough, she was *very* hot.

A few hours of sleep helped Luna to get her thoughts tidied up. She had the question of who screamed, and everything else that had happened that year, yet without Louis or Coco, Luna knew that she had no way of translating anything that had happened.

"Psssst, Hey, Luna?" Said a rather usual Coco voice. Excitedly, Luna chucked the curtains back and saw something not exciting. Not exciting at all. Coco was lying there, grinning, alive. But what injuries she had were severely punishing. Her head seemed to be cracked open, blood searing through the bandages, her nose was practically hanging off like a door off its hinges, and her left hand was gone!

"Co! What? What happened to you?" Luna replied, all happiness drained out of her soul.

It took Coco a while to process what she had said, but then she answered, "Oh! This stuff? Well, I was walking down the corridor to visit you, then Jasmine hopped along and sliced my head then walked away, as the blood covered my face. I'm assuming Katie, used a complicated wing movement to slice my hand so I couldn't attach my emergency wings, then one of the three, probably Jennifer, came and used another, rare, yet obviously effective movement to chop off my poor, innocent little nose, the little"

(Coco said a rather rude word I mustn't repeat). "I collapsed on the floor like a doll, and then ended up here." She seemed rather calm telling this story.

"What in the name of Rogererare did they do that for? I mean, if they were really angry then surely they would of came to me right? I mean, they hate me! Not *you*!" Luna raged.

"I know. But don't worry, it's only the fourth time."

"*WHAT*"

"Yeah, didn't I tell you?"

"NO! You didn't! Jasmine, Katie, and Jennifer have done this to you *four* times?"

"No, not them, but. Y'know, being homeless and stuff, you get attacked sometimes."

Lunas stomach churned, she felt uncomfortable talking about this subject with Coco. She blinked roughly.

"Its fine you know. All my friends think of me as a stupid idiot every time I mention it, I'm happy you understand." Coco replied. For the first time in her life, Luna saw Coco punch her pillow in anger.

"Are you alright?" Luna asked tentatively.

"Yes, but I just wish I had my own room, in my own house, with my *whole* family."

As Luna listened, she thought of something. "Coco, I understand, but, but out of pure curiosity, if you don't, umm, live with your parents, how come you got a Christmas gift from them?"

"Oh, I knew this would come up. Rachel knits them and pretends they're from Mum and Dad so that if anyone reads them that isn't me, then they won't get suspicious - what is that!" Mrs Penny barged into the hall with a tray floating over her head, holding two, what seemed like, drills, and several needles.

"Right you two, Copper, Wheezleberry, one surgery each, and some needles. I'll do Miss Wheezleberry first." She wandered casually over to Coco and picked up the drill type thing, then closed the curtains. There was a large AAAH, AAH, aah ah. Then nothing, just nice ah's and ooh's. Then once a few moments had passed. Mrs Penny jogged tiredly over to Lunas bed.

The drilling was nowhere near as painful as expected, but felt quite soothing. The ominous feeling of the needles however, which there were five of, was extraordinarily painful, one in the arm, one on the leg, one in the side, one in the cheek, and one somewhere else.

Once the needles and drills were complete, Coco had fallen asleep, so Luna knew it might be her only opportunity to get a complete period of rest.

When she awoke, everything seemed normal, (well, as normal as possible at that time), except Coco was staring at her through desperate eyes, holding a piece of paper and putting it in Lunas direction. She took it, then read it through;

Hi Luna,

Just letting you know, if me and you are both, umm, temporarily held up, then the only person left is Louis, to, y,know sort things out, but he's possessed. So, were kinda doomed. I'm extraordinarily worried.

Your friend,

Coco

Luna almost cried with joy at this. She knew that at least Coco was feeling the same as her. On the back, she wrote;

Hi Coco,

I understand, I feel the same way, if I could choose how this year went, I can promise you, I wouldn't of even imagined it like this. I'm so so sorry, we'll work things out, I swear.

Your friend,

Luna

Coco read this through, nodded at Luna, and grinned. Then she picked up a random newspaper and began to read, Luna watched for a minute, trying to see what was on the page, then she spotted some more on Cocos chair, "Hey! Pass me one!" Coco flung a newspaper at Luna and she spun through the pages, looking at headlines, *'Fliers In Front Of Fish'*. *'Things Not To Do During A School Class'*. *'Gold Mining In Europe'*. Until something caught Lunas eye as she turned to page 15. *'Criminals To Watch Out For, The New Book To Trend!'* Luna read;

'Female writer Zoe Flann has only just released a new book! 3000 pages all about who to watch out for! Murderers, Burglars, Shoplifters!

If you're a fan of danger, then be sure to speed over to those stores all over town before they sell out! Get your copy now!

"Its nothing, people already know who most of these people are, I just wanted a personal record for myself, nothing to worry about, they'll stick about for a while if you ask me." Quotes author Zoe Flann, although others have opposite opinions.

'Waste of money! Nothing in there to interest a rat! Hate this stupid book, zero out of ten!' Quotes buyer Finland Drackstone.

'Loving it! On chapter four hundred and one already! Very handy! Definitely recommend it to anyone looking for some shillings! You can get quite the bucket load for catching criminals. Great book, love it!' Quotes buyer Poppy Tittani.

'I've seen better, but it's worth the money in my opinion. Definitely worse out there.' Quotes buyer Anthony Ho Shangleberry.

Available at any shops dear Dukestown. Only £15.99 UK, €17.49 US.

Includes long stories of the history of these criminals! Buy now!

Lunas body boiled with excitement. "Coco, *look*!" She showed the page to Coco, who's eyes darted across it.

"Nice one! Keep the paper, I don't know where 'Dukestown' is though. We'll have to read about it. Anyway, Mrs Penny said I should, 'Save my head and rest.' So, I'm going to sleep, see you in a few hours. Night, or, noon." Coco laid down and Luna kept sitting.

Luna heard a "Meow." She looked over her bed and saw all of the four cats sitting on the floor.

"Aw hello, hi! Wait... I haven't fed you in like, days. Umm." Luna said, she picked a random fish out of the tank on her desk and she threw it to the cats. Once the kittens had shared the poor salmon equally, Luna picked up each cat one by one and placed them on the bed sheets. "So, I need names for you guys, don't I. Umm-" She picked up the pure white kitten, and said, "I'll name you, Kayla." (Luna had absolutely no idea why). She picked up the larger white cat and said, "Hmm, I'll name you Alice." (These names were completely random). She picked up the tiny kitten with a ginger ear, then said, "Belgium. Definitely, don't know why, you just look like a Belgium." And lastly, the pure ginger cat, "Your name is obviously Ginger... well guys, I'm afraid you're going to have to spend the night here with me. I have some spare pillows luckily."

She threw a few spare cushions on the floor and the cats took one each, and curled up.

Luna drifted off to sleep, but when she awoke, she was shocked to see Louis, parts of his face still silhouetted and blackened, but he was returning back to usual, and he was sitting on the bottom of her bed by her feet, tears dampening his face.

"Oh my God! You're, you're, not dead!" He yelled, waking up Coco, who grumbled.

"Nope, not dead, just a broken neck." Luna replied. She only just realised that Louis was not alone, a few other students were crowded around the clearing in the curtains.

"Hey! Louis! I'm here too y'know! I could get a, 'You're not dead!' too!" Coco yelled, as the rain pounded against all windows.

"Oh, umm. Yes, yes just a second, Luna did I tell you I got a note that we both didn't go to the - ow! Sorry Luna." He said, he began rubbing the blackened parts of his face which had unrecognisable scars on them.

"Are you ok?" Asked Luna.

"Er, yes… just an after effect of possess ability. You know." he replied. Luna nodded appreciatively. "Well, what I was saying was we both didn't go to the Winghinging tryouts."

"Oh gosh! We didn't did we? Ugh!" Luna smacked herself on the head.

Before she could say goodbye, Louis was already sitting on Coco's bed looking after her.

Luna, without thinking, went to join them on Cocos bed.

"Er, guys?" She murmured tentatively, "What do we know so far? Rogererare told me to ask you guys how much we know about the strange series of events over the last six months."

Coco swallowed, "We know Barney is possessed, we know he's a… a… killer-" She looked on the verge of tears. "I'm so sorry Luna. I could of saved her, but, I didn't… but I swear, I tried, I really did. But something… something got inside me and stopped me… I'm… I'm so… sorry."

"Yes, you're right he is. But, but what are you talking about… you could have saved her?"

Louis looked at her, he begun a very difficult multitask. He tried to comfort Coco, her unavoidably ginger hair hung over his blackened arm as he hugged her, meanwhile, he explained, "Well, well when… when we went, to the basement, the... the man, he strangled Alex with ivy, Coco knew an anti-ivy wing pronunciation, but before she could say it, Alex... she, she stopped breathing."

Luna was visited with an urge to throw herself on the ground and have a fit. But she wouldn't let her friends think a fool of her.

Louis had read her mind, "Its alright to cry, it really is."

Luna couldn't help it, she joined the hug. A few seconds later, an unfamiliar child spoke.

CHAPTER TEN: BREAK IN

The boy was dark haired and dark eyed. His hair was the same shade of dark as Luna's, and he was holding a letter. He just stood there staring at Luna.

"Um, hi?" Luna said. The boy jumped. She tried to take the letter but he winced, this told her it wasn't her letter. Coco and Louis took no notice of the boy whatsoever.

"The galloping stallion may meet you at the special place." He said, Luna asked what he meant, but he just repeated himself, "The galloping stallion may meet you at the special place." He said it once more, then vanished in a cloud of dust.

"Umm, did you guys see that?" She said to her two emotional friends.

"See what?" Coco replied worriedly.

"That boy."

"Huh? What boy? No?"

Louis joined in, "There was no boy Luna."

"YES! That boy there." She motioned to the location where the boy had been but her friends stared at her in astonishment. "He, he said the galloping stallion will meet me at the special place. Any ideas?"

"Well it's obvious, you lunatic, get it, Luna-tic?" Coco said. She got only blank expressionless faces back. "Sorry."

Louis had that face which means he had suddenly thought of something. Coco nudged him and he revealed his thoughts, "Luna, did your dad have any... nicknames... while he was here?"

"What the... I mean, um, no, I... maybe?"

"Let's go to the-"

"Library." The girls finished his sentence. The three of them got up and tiptoed to the door until Mrs Penny stopped them.

"I'm not even going to ask, but whatever it is, *No!* Not without a worker, not with maladies like this! Possession Burns, Lost hand, broken neck, cracked head and broken nose! You still think I'll let you go wandering around the corridors in that state! Yeah right!" She yelled.

"You come with us then! We're only looking up Luna's-" Coco kicked him, "-Hairstyle."

"Oh, alright then! Be careful though you three!"

"Hairstyle?" Luna asked as they limped to the library.

"Yeah, well, what would you of said?" He replied.

"Anything but *hairstyle!*" Coco jeered, in a whisper.

They arrived at the library, and Mrs Penny rested on an armchair. They scurried behind a shelf and began a whisper.

"Can one of you guys read, I'm not good with my left hand." Said Coco, she held up her lonely wrist.

"I will. Luna, you find the book, remember, 'Tragic Deaths Of Winged Beauties Most Wonderous Students'. Year two. Coco, you keep watch, I'll read." Louis whispered. They all set off in different directions.

After a few minutes Luna had searched her way to find that particular book, and she took it to Coco and Louis, who were sitting on levitating beanbags.

Once Luna had handed him the book, Louis peeped round the corner to check that no one was there, then began to whisper the contents to the girls.

"Chapter nineteen, Vicky and Charlie Copper. Vicky Runder was a charming young girl, who's eyes where as blue as the sky, and dark hair alike the black silk of the year five wings. She grew up in a wealthy village by the name of, 'Dirington' in the state of Dukestown, with her mother Molly, and her father Alexander, with her two winglets, and non-flier dog. Vicky was a beautiful teenager, who kept her hair from her childhood, she went to the school Winged Beauties Boarding School For Children With The Gift, up to year seven, where she mysteriously disappeared, along with her boyfriend Charlie Copper. She grew to be a Winglet trainer, and married Charlie fourteen years after the disappearance. She then gave birth to her beautiful young daughter Luna, who is now four years old and living with her grandparents. Charlie Copper was forever known as the Hero Troublemaker, or The Galloping Stallion, for his independence and great speed and courage. He would always sacrifice anything he had for others, and grew to be wise and heroic. He too, went to Winged Beauties

Boarding School For Children With The Gift, and met young Vicky in year five, as Winghinging partners. He grew to be captain of the British Ravens Winghinging team, and once his gorgeous daughter was born, soon gave every second of every day towards her, by resigning from his job and looking after her while his wife was working. The two of them were tragically killed by an unidentified flying object, and are now buried in Frandel Cemetary in Dirington. They will always be remembered for Vicky's cleverness and protection of her daughter, and Charlie's bravery and courage he used to save others' lives."

"You have your mother's hair." Coco exclaimed.

"And your father's eyes, well, I think." Louis continued, reading the blurb.

"I… but, my dad is dead." Luna said miserably.

Coco looked at her feet, Louis rolled his eyes, "You two don't use your ears do you. I might have been possessed, but I can remember things, your dad said his body was in Marig Hospital For Winged Injuries! Barney must have healed him! Well, not Barney, whoever he has possessed has."

Oh my god! Thought Luna, inside her own head.

"Where is the special place though? I mean, my old… no, no it can't be." Luna said.

"I think so, yeah." Louis answered.

"What am I missing here?" Coco asked angrily.

"LUNA'S OLD HOME!" Said Louis and Luna in unison.

"Oh you've got to be kidding me." Coco answered.

"Nope." Grinned Luna.

"Well, we better leave ASAP. Like, after Winghinging class. There are only two weeks left of the school term. So, pack up girls were going on an adventure!" Louis said.

"Oh my god! Your right! How on earth am I going to tell my siblings about this?" Coco moaned.

"No idea! But no time to stop and wonder. Let's get these injuries sorted out before class then set off." Luna repeated.

"Oh, don't think that getting our injuries sorted out will be painless. If you've ever read 'Curious Cures' by Minnie Psydoff, then you'll know that I'll need to get my blackened areas cut off by using a year seven movement, then they attach new flesh. Coco will need extreme treatment, which tastes a *bit* tangy, actually, not a bit, a *lot*. And Luna, well, a flying wheelchair." Louis reminded them.

"Oh" (explicit) "I forgot about that, will we bring Anna, and Skye? Or will they keep our cover?" Coco queried.

"I think they should come with us. Y'know, Anna knows about flying injuries, and Skye, well, she will feel left out surely?" Luna said, Louis raised his eyebrows in despair. "Well, you know stuff too."

"*MRS PENNY!*" Louis squealed.

"Yes dear?" Came a shout from behind the shelf.

"Er... me, and Coco and Luna are deciding that we would like to have our curing operations now, before class. Please." He answered hopefully.

"Well, if your all entirely sure, then let's get back to the wing quickly, and maybe a little snack too?" She replied.

"That sounds lovely." Louis said politely, he gave the girls a thumbs up, and the three of them burst upwards, and ran towards the door.

Once they had arrived they all laid down on their beds, (Louis' directly across from Coco, and diagonal to Luna), and Mrs Penny scurried over to Louis' bed, closed the curtains, then there was silence. The two girls listened carefully, nothing happened until a few minutes into the operation, when for the first time they could remember, they heard Louis *cry*!

"Is he alright? She's not... not *hurting* him is she?" Coco said worriedly.

"Remember, he warned us that it wouldn't be painless, he's getting new flesh sewn to his head for goodness sake! He'll be fine." Luna reassured her, although he was very upset.

There was a beautifully reassuring 'All done!' And Mrs Penny opened the curtains once more. Louis was sitting up, with a fully normal face and nothing but a stitch on his forehead. He still looked wary though.

The nurse hurriedly jogged over to Coco, then told her what she was about to taste, "This medicine, according to the scientists, is legitimately eleven times as hot as a ghost pepper. Are you sure you want to do this Miss Wheezleberry?"

Coco looked worried enough that it was a possibility that she was going to say no, but she inhaled solemnly, and nodded. Mrs Penny shrugged, and took a spoon, tapped it, then the sides of it sprouted minute wings, and she clicked her fingers, the spoon dug into the bowl and returned with a watery substance, then shoved itself roughly into Coco's mouth.

She blushed bright scarlet, her eyes widened, and she pleaded for water. Mrs Penny handed her a cup, and she gobbled it down with a loud gulp. She then drained all colour, although all of her body parts had returned to their rightful places.

Then it was Luna's turn to shiver, the levitating chair sped towards her at at least forty miles per hour. It then stopped right in front of her. Mrs Penny jogged over, and a random hand dislocated from the nurses, it flapped its pinkie and thumb in an uncomfortably awkward fashion, and grabbed her neck brace violently. Then it flew off and Luna felt the bone in her neck again!

"Right, hop in the chair young lady, and don't move whilst I fix it to fly back here in exactly one hour." Mrs Penny demanded. Luna sat comfortably in the chair, peacefully, until Mrs Penny made the chair vibrate so much that Luna swung around, no different from a jelly snake. Then it stopped. Luna had injured her ankle, until Mrs Penny gave it a twist, and a loud pop. Then it was fine!

"Right, you three, no more injuries or I won't treat you!" Mrs Penny threatened, then hurried them out the door.

The three of them scurried, (or in Lunas case, flew) across the hall to Professor Fire's classroom, not talking at all, as they were all thinking wisely about what to pack for the journey.

"You're, late. Miss Copper, Miss Wheezleberry, Mr Lochsmith, that's a warning!" Professor Fire announced to everyone. He looked abnormally normal. He was wearing an all-in-one black jumpsuit, and his hair was white blonde.

They apologised and sat down, Luna parked her chair neatly in the corner.

"Okay, now that *everyone* has arrived, we may start the test, to see what you know so far about our sport. Turn your pages." He was so firm, that nobody needed telling twice. Everyone picked up a quill, and began.

Louis whizzed through all of them in five minutes and, as normal, was the first one to hand it in. Coco sat biting her nails and Luna was barely better. The first question was, 'Which famous player scored the winning goal in the match between British Eagles and Chinese Ravens? A. John Cameron. B. Murray Blackburn. C. Jo Stewart' Luna hadn't heard of any of these and randomly circled B. Question two was, 'What is the winning ball? A. Coka. B. Coga. C. Yoga.' Luna knew that it was A.

She quickly circled A. The rest of the questions were simple, except from questions, fifty-four and thirty-one. Once Luna had handed hers in, the strangest thing happened, the window behind the teacher burst violently and something, or someone, flew through it, along with around six others. They were too quick to see, but were blurs of black and red.

"Out of the classrooms! Immediately! Gather to the Grand Hall! Immediately!" Professor Fire demanded. Louis and Coco were holding hands with fright, and Luna hurried through the crowds of bothered students to reach them. Louis was trying to pull Coco off her seat, but she was rooted to the spot.

"Coco! Please!" Louis begged, and she looked up at Luna and ran with them. Everyone was sitting at the wooden benches in the Grand Hall, and Rogererare was standing on a platform raised up by two cyan wings.

"Now! All lessons are cancelled! All students must gather in fives! Then all travel to one building with their parents! Immediately! Am I clear?" Rogererare said angrily, as students and pupils were too busy sobbing, or chatting.

"We'd better stick together. We will go to my house, it'll be safer there. For the moment. Skye and Anna?" Louis whispered. The girls nodded, and they jogged or wheeled over to where Skye was sobbing delicately and Anna was comforting her deeply. "Come on. I've contacted James. He's on his way. We will collect your parents shortly." He informed them. Anna and Skye nodded and stood up.

CHAPTER ELEVEN: COTTAGE GRIEF

A few moments later, piles of parents gathered into the hall. One of which a man, with a small child on his shoulders.

Louis tapped them all and pointed, then ran towards the man. "James!"

The man hugged him and said, "Have you got your four? Quickly! The Devils are near."

"Yes, this is Luna, Coco, Anna, and Skye. Are they actually Devils?" Louis asked.

"Yes. Alright, have you five gotten your wings stored in a pocket somewhere?" James asked politely but eagerly. They all took them out from their pockets and attached them. Apart from Luna who's chair was doing all the work. "Brilliant. Right, we best get going. We will collect your families soon. Yes, well done, Luna? So sorry hon, but yes, your chair will fly you there. Eve, you ready?"

"Yes daddy!" Yelled the small child. Louis jogged over and picked her up.

"I'll take her James. Its OK." Louis announced. James nodded and they stepped cautiously onto the balcony outside.

"On three, jump, and follow me. Its not far." James instructed specifically.

"One!"

"Two!"

"Three!"

All six of them jumped and Luna flew off. They saw James' glittering violet wings heading South. They flew after him.

After around fifteen minutes of going right and left the right again, a small cottage appeared on the valley.

"House!" Cried Eve.

"Careful you five, its a hard landing." James warned them, he landed himself and tapped his pocket. A split ring flew out and started to unlock the front door. He opened it to let everyone inside. It was so stuffed full of books and old magazines that you had to wind your way through the stacks.

"Cool! I wish I had this many books!" Coco exclaimed.

"Thank you sweetie. You lot go upstairs. Me and Eve will prepare a snack for you in a while. Oh! And Lou, check for new clothes and pyjamas, for all of you please." James replied.

Anna, Skye, Coco, Luna and Louis all trotted up the stairs. (Luna found it rather difficult seeing as she was in a chair, although her friends heaved her up) and entered a room with the letters LL carved into a small plaque on the door. They all plunged into armchairs and beanbags and Lunas chair disappeared. She landed in a heap on the floor. Anna pulled her up.

"My old Foster Mum had a thing about keeping childhood clothes. I'll go rummaging in there for clothes for you guys and I'll change whilst I'm at it, make yourselves at home." Louis said, whist opening the door and walking out.

A few minutes had passed of looking around and looking at photos of little Louis on the mantelpiece, until Louis returned. Wearing blue and white striped pyjamas and carrying a pile of clothes which he dropped on the floor.

"Take your pick." He said, then plopped down on his bed cross-legged. Each girl picked out a couple of items of clothing and hurried out of the room to change.

Coco and Luna arrived back first, Coco wearing a pastel blue top and magenta joggers, and Luna a green onesie. Coco settled on the other side of the bed and Luna settled herself into a furry beanbag. Louis was sitting on his pillow, holding one knee, and resting a book on his thigh. He didn't acknowledge that the girls were there.

Skye and Anna arrived soon afterwards, wearing matching purple tops and leggings, and breaking the silence. "My mum and big brother Adam are arriving tomorrow morning." Skye whispered. Louis snapped the book shut and laid it violently next to him.

"That's great Skye. Really, great." He answered impatiently. Coco and Luna glanced at each other. There was an ominous feeling around the room.

"Same with my mum and dad, they insisted they came to me tonight. They are on their way." Anna said, joining the conversation.

Louis nodded. "What about you Coco? When are your siblings arriving?"

"Oh, er, tomorrow, one o'clock." She answered nervously. No one spoke, something was wrong, that was definite. Although James had called them all down.

They all sprinted downstairs, and James had laid out a roast chicken dinner for seven. James, Eve, Louis, Anna, Skye, Coco, and Luna, all sat down and dug in. There was a chap on the door, and James ran round a mountain of non-fiction American Histories and opened it. A glamorous woman, with white-blonde hair and green eyes, and a tall man with a large moustache entered. Anna stood up and ran over to them.

"Mum! Dad! Your here!" She yelped excitedly.

"Hello beautiful. Hi, I'm Millie, and this is my fiancé Luke. We are Anna's parents." Said the woman, shaking James' hand.

"Wonderful to meet you. I can pull up a few more chairs I suppose." James added. He rushed over to a smaller table with a glass of coffee sitting on it, and he pulled two wooden chairs to the dining table. Millie and Luke sat down.

"Well, what drinks do we have up for grabs, I'm dehydrated from the flight." Said Luke.

"Oh erm." James stuttered. "Water. Or, or a glass of wine, if, if you prefer."

"Oh, I could go for a glass actually. Thanks mate." Luke answered.

"Water please." Millie replied, sophisticatedly.

"Right then. Eight waters and a wine, right." James whispered, and he hurried into the kitchen.

"Well, you four must be Anna's new friends. Very nice." Millie exclaimed.

"Yes. Yeah, I'm Coco." Coco answered.

"Luna."

"Louis."

"Skye."

"Lovely. Well, I don't want my little darling staying up too late. Finish up soon children then you best be off to bed." Millie ordered.

"Yes Miss." Louis shivered. For some reason all five of them munched quickly.

In ten awkwardly silent minutes, all five of them had finished. They hurried into the dark hall after saying goodnight, and Louis muttered, "phohsphorieia." And the very tips of his wings lit up.

"Come. Luna, Coco, there's something I need to tell you. Skye, Anna, there's two floating mattresses in my room." Louis whispered. Everyone nodded suspiciously. Anna and Skye scurried into the bedroom, and Louis, followed by Coco, and Luna, wandered down the hall. Louis' wings illuminated the pathway. He swerved alarmingly around a pile of Eve's princess books, and muttered, "erebos" and darkness swallowed them once more. He reached for each girls hand and pulled them through a door. He switched the light on, it was a walk-in wardrobe, although, without the clothes.

"Er, where are we?" Coco asked, both eagerly and terrifyingly.

"I don't know, but I have two things that I *need* to tell you two." Louis muttered.

"Well, we are in your house, so." Coco replied.

"Alright, alright, we are in my Foster mum's old wardrobe. But, the point is, do you want to know now? Or get some sleep first?" He answered, clearly flustered.

"Now, please." The girls answered in unison.

"Alright, so, firstly, I have a plan on how to go to your dad, Luna. Although it might be dangerous, and I can't promise that all three of us will come back alive. I'm willing to take that risk, for your dad's sake, and yours." He answered.

"I, I, I don't, don't know, I mean, Coco? Are, are you-"

"Yes, I will risk that if it means you can meet your dad after eleven years of never seeing him." Coco said, honestly.

Luna was shocked. Her friends were willing to risk their lives, for her?

"All in favour of Luna going to meet her father please raise your hands." Louis announced, Coco and Louis' hands were raised. Luna felt guilty, but tentatively raised her own hand. "Its settled. Well, tomorrow, I get to go down to the lake, to go to the bookshop, I'm guessing that you two would be allowed to come too, but instead, we can go to Dirington, I looked it up, you lived at 1 Roasi Street. James, *can't know.* He'd ground me for life if he found out I'd gone that far away." Louis explained.

"What about Skye and Anna?" Coco queried.

"Ah, leave that to me." Louis said with a smirk.

"Your second thing?" Luna asked with a nod of agreement.

"The Devils. If I can get any further details, I will tell you, but so far, I only know what they do. Not how they got here or anything. Devils, are horrible things, really, horrible. They are normal fliers with replaced, enchanted flesh. The enchantments mean that they cannot get hurt or injured or killed. The enchantment also makes their skin red. They wear black cloaks and their wings are invisible, they just float. They always travel in groups of nine, mysteriously, and they grab you, knock you unconscious, swallow all your blood, and once it's all gone, rip you in half. They feed on grief, on despair and depression. They're who came to the castle."

"Wait, your saying, that if Rogererare hadn't evacuated us all, then some of us would be teared in half?" Coco repeated.

"Yes, that's why we travelled in fives, so we have witnesses of any accidents. Although, the Devils are on a close watch over the country, so that's one, of the many, reasons why it'll be dangerous to go to Roasi Street." Louis answered.

Lunas stomach back flipped. She felt sick, there was a scream, someone dived onto her and chucked her out of the way, someone landed next to her, there was a bang on the door, no one could enter, or exit.

"Guys, guys sit up! Out the window, *NOW!*" Louis screamed, he grabbed Luna's hand. They opened a window and jumped.

The three of them crashed down in a heap on the ground. Louis heaved both of them up. Anna, Millie, Luke, Eve, James, and all of the pets flew and ran out of the house, it was only then that Luna realised the cottage was burning down to foundations.

"Wait, where's Skye? Mum, where's Skye? *Mum! Where's Skye!*" Anna cried, no one answered, "WHERE IS SHE! MUM! MUM WHERE, IS, SKYE!"

Anna's chin wobbled, her eyes watered. She looked back at the burnt building, "She, she couldn't, no, no, no! Skye is out here! Skye! Skye?" Anna pleaded.

The firemen arrived, they sprayed down the building with carbon dioxide. Anna sobbed into her Mother's sweater. Louis, Luna, and Coco, all comforted her.

"Well, I'm sure I've got a tent stored in the wingwalk, I'll go get it." James added politely. He flew up to a platform directly above the broken household. He returned with a four-man tent. He began to put it up.

"Anna, please darling, eat, please." Her mother begged, but Anna refused. James had put the tent up and set out some pillows and blankets, along with Eve's cuddly llama, and a few saveable books. Louis, Eve, James, Millie, Luke, and Coco entered. Luna however, sat down next to her grieving friend, who was sitting in the dirt, holding what looked like an old locket.

"Anna, are you alright?" Luna asked.

"No, Skye can't of died, she's, well, intelligent, and she wouldn't just sit there and burn. She must have gotten a fright and, ran away or something. I just don't believe that she's dead." Anna muttered.

"What's that locket?" Luna asked.

"The fireman, his name was Jackson, he found this in the rubble. Its Skye's friendship locket. She never took it off." Anna answered.

"I really think we should get in, its cold out here, let's get some sleep." Luna recommended.

"Fine." Anna grudged. They quietly tiptoed into the tent, Millie and Luke were sleeping under a furry black blanket, and James was under an identical one, hugging Eve, who was cuddling her soft llama. Louis was huddled in a corner, Coco leaning on him and sleeping, and reading a book. He looked up and waved his available hand at the two of them, Anna hugged him. Luna got under a fluffy purple blanket and hugged Anna on the other side.

It took Luna a while to fall asleep, although once all of her friends were dreaming, she closed her eyes... She was in the corridor at Winged Beauties, a man with a blurred face chumming her. She saw Coco and Louis' dead bodies on the floor, she walked by like nothing had happened, she continued walking until Rogererare gave her a hug at the end of the corridor. There was a door that opened gradually at her every step. She walked in, it was a HQ. It had the letters B.N.B painted on the damp walls. There were a lot of people playing cards and drinking beer, there was a man at the other side of the room, he waved at her...

"Luna! Luna wake up! Its quarter past nine!" Coco was pushing her, her hair was tied back in a ponytail, and she was wearing a denim jacket. Louis was eating a bowl of Flying Fantasies cereal, and Anna was sat miserably in a corner spinning her spoon around her bowl. The adults and Eve were eating bread and butter, and Coco sat down next to Louis and continued eating her Flying Fantasies.

"Your bowl's there Luna." Louis pointed to a fresh, milky bowl of cereal. Luna sat up and pulled it over.

"You were pretty sleepy huh? We woke up an hour ago, you have a jumpsuit drying outside to go and change into." Louis explained. Eve shuffled over to them, still carrying her llama.

"Do you guys like what I changed Fred into?" She asked. She held up her llama, it was wearing a bright pink tutu, and a black and white shirt with the text: KEEP CALM AND CARRY ON.

"Lovely Eve." Louis answered.

"Beautiful, very pretty." Coco lied.

"Nice!" Luna fibbed.

"It's OK." Anna answered.

Eve hurried over back to James.

"Oh! Luna, I forgot to tell you, at Winged Beauties I found this little guy on the stairs, one of his legs came off but he still sings;"

"I love you, you love me

I like nice hot yummy tea

You are kind, don't I know

Your nice bow is quite a show."

It was Toffee! Luna gasped. As Louis had said, he was one legged, but that didn't matter. Suddenly, Anna screamed.

"What is the matter gorgeous?" Millie asked.

"I, I was trying to text Skye, and, she replied! She sent this." Anna held her wing up.

[Anna Rigmont] Skye? You there? : (

[Skye Macdonaldson] 190200, 190200, 190200 190200, 190200

Luna felt boggled.

"It might be a phone number, try it." Coco recommended. Anna typed in the numbers on the 'Add Number +' and called it.

"Bonjour?" It said.

"Er, yeah hi, do you know Skye Macdonaldson?" Anna answered.

"Je ne comprends pas."

"No, er, Skye, Macdonaldson."

"ALLEZ-VOUS EN!" The caller hung up.

"Er, maybe not." Coco joked.

"They were French. I speak a little bit of French." Louis informed them.

"What did they say to me?" Anna asked.

"Well, at first they said hello, then when you asked them, they said, I don't understand, and when you repeated yourself, they said, go away." He answered truthfully.

"Ugh. I feel offended now." Anna moaned.

"It might be a date. Its only five days away!" Louis said.

"Oh! Then it must be Valentine's day. Shame we aren't at school." Luna exclaimed, looking at the pile of chrysanthemums sitting next to Millie. Coco blushed.

"Well, speaking of flowers, I got all four of, I mean, three of you a posy." He handed Anna, Coco, and Luna each a little pink flower. Anna put hers in her hair, and Coco copied. Luna did the same.

Anna tapped them. She showed her wing.

[Anna Rigmont] Anything else?

[Skye Macdonaldson] Wolverine Alley

Anna grinned. She then didn't. Skye texted something else.

[Skye Macdonaldson] I die

"I told you guys that it was a date!" Louis bragged.

"What do you mean, it's a date?" Luna asked, intrigued.

"Wolverine Alley. Nineteenth of February two thousand. Skye will die!" He whispered.

Anna gasped. Lunas eyes widened.

"James? Are we still going to the bookshop?" Louis asked with hope.

"Jolly well yes! We need more books!" James answered.

"I won't come. I want to try and find out more information." Anna said.

"Okay, I'll go change, then we'll leave." Luna said, and she exited the tent. There was indeed a red jumpsuit on the ground, and some boots.

Luna changed, and invited Coco and Louis outside. Louis exited, and Coco followed him out.

"Wow! It's so beautiful out here. Look at the sun! Actually, no, don't look at the sun." Coco said, rubbing her eyes.

"Well, let's start flying." Louis said, with a hint of amusement. They spread their wings, and jumped off the hill.

CHAPTER TWELVE: ROASI STREET

The journey took around an hour. Coco had put her enchanted wing paint on her wings so she was ahead of the other two. As they passed a field, they decided to land.

Coco leapt up, spitting hair and grass out of her mouth. Luna returned upwards wiping down her jumpsuit, and Louis stood up, his T-shirt covered in dirt. As they walked over to the sign noting, 'Welcome to Dukestown' The girls noticed that Louis was limping.

"Louis, is your leg alright?" Coco asked.

"Yeah, I think I just scratched it when I landed in the dirt, I'm OK, Luna. Roasi Street is just on this corner." He pointed to a side street on the side of the road.

Everyone seemed very happy in Dukestown. They were wearing sun hats and chatting. People were selling bread and vegetables at stands, there were many antique and clothing shops as well. The houses where very old fashioned. They were large and had intricate, wooden designs around them. There were a few winglets, and cwingers, and a few non-flier pets like dogs and cats wandering the streets. The sun smothered them, making their eyes glisten.

They turned a corner. It was a gorgeous street. The sign noting the name of the street was surrounded by roses and sunflowers. Where number one should have stood, there was an empty gap.

"Ah, it's been queeled!" Louis announced angrily, staring at the gap.

"Excuse me?" Luna queried.

"Queeled, its basically, well, when a houses owner, or one of it's owners passes away, the house floats fifteen miles in the sky, that's why widows have such a hard time." Coco answered, "I can get there in a minute, if I just held your hands, we'd be there in a tick."

She reached for Luna and Louis' hands, and jumped, they were going upwards at high speed.

"Holy cricket! I didn't know you were that good at ups Coco!" Louis complimented.

"Thanks." Coco said, blushing.

Luna looked at her, Coco looked back, she smiled.

"*COCO! WATCH OUT!*" Louis screamed.

The three of them bashed on the bottom of the wooden floor, hitting their heads.

Coco flew to where the patio was sat. They sat down, on the cold, damp, stone floor, and looked at the sky.

"It really is beautiful out here." Luna said.

"Yeah, always is. Especially out on this side of the country." Louis answered.

It started to rain. "Oh, we'd better get in. It's raining." Coco recommended. They stood up and walked into the building. As they entered, the lights flickered, making an ominous vibe.

There was a bang upstairs, and a tall man, with hazelnut hair, glasses, and a perfectly fitted striped suit, hurried down the stairs, he saw the trio and stopped in his tracks.

"My darling daughter." He said, he ran down the hall and picked up Luna. "You came! You, you really came!" Tears poured down his cheeks, he stroked Luna's dark hair, and touched her face. "It's really you, it's really, really you!"

"Of course it's me!" Luna yelled. She felt so joyful.

"I knew it! I *knew it!*" He screamed.

"Hello! Mr Copper!" Louis said politely.

"Oh, it's a pleasure to meet you in person! I've been watching you two too! I can read thoughts! Never hide your true feelings! Both of you!" He yelled. Coco looked embarrassed.

"Get upstairs now, get upstairs, I'll make us all a cup of tea and some toast eh? There is a lounge upstairs, off you go." Charlie motioned them up the stairs. They wandered the hall until they spotted a large room with silky sofas and a lovely wooden coffee table.

"You just met your dad." Louis said, oblivious to the fact that everyone knew that.

"I, I know. I, can't, can't believe it! I guess, its just, the fact that I'm, not an, an orphan, it just, just really gave me a good feeling you know?" She replied.

"Should he come back home with us?" Louis asked.

"Definitely. I don't think staying here is a very intelligent idea, he needs-" Luna was interrupted by a mighty crash downstairs.

All three of them jumped up, and sprinted downstairs. In the kitchen, the knife was still covered in butter, the window was smashed, and there was a mug on the ground. But more importantly, Charlie was gone!

"Dad?" Luna yelled, no one answered. It was empty, too empty. The three of them stood, looking around and not speaking a word.

"Luna." Coco said, the others jumped, "Luna, Luna what is that, that, that thing, on your arm, what is that?"

"What thing?" Luna answered, she didn't dare look at her arm.

"Luna, look at your arm. Please, look at your arm." Louis joined in.

Luna looked at her forearm, the words were carving themselves into her flesh, it bled slightly. 'I CAN SEE YOU. RUN!'

"Why do we ru~" She stopped her own voice. With shock, Coco had disappeared. She hadn't moved, walked, jumped, anything, yet she was gone.

"COCO!" Louis yelled.

"I thought I told you to run. Run, now. And go, go to Wolverine Alley. Run there, I can see you…I can… Always… See you…" Said a hooded figure standing at the doorway. He too, vanished.

"I know what he's doing. That *idiot*! That foul, evil little *idiot*!" Louis screamed, he was so filled with rage, that he didn't hear Luna.

"Louis! Louis! What is he doing? And who is 'he' anyway?" Luna queried.

"Barney! The *real* one! He wants to kill you so he's captured everyone you love! At Wolverine Alley! He's luring you! So that he can strike. Luna, remember this. If I go too, remember. You have to go, if it means dying, do it, you are *strong* Luna, you can outrun him, I know you can Luna, I have faith in you, our lives, depend on it." He replied.

"Why does he want to kill me?" She replied.

"That's the part I don't know."

"Louis, Louis because were being honest, I had a dream, back at the tent, I had a dream. I was walking into a headquarters. It said B.N.B. But, you and Coco were dead."

Louis didn't speak, he stared into her eyes. "Barney Nicho Bubwul, B.N.B. You need to go there, and I know where it is."

"Where?" Luna pleaded.

"Bloodhill Manor. It's on Wolverine Alley. I was stupid, I knew that Wolverine Alley was otherwise known as Death Street. Barney owns it, he lives in Bloodhill Manor. You need to go Luna, you need to." He answered.

"If that is true. Then does that mean, does that mean the part of the dream where you and Coco were dead, does that mean that that's true too?" Luna asked.

Louis stared at her, he blinked and a teardrop dampened his face.

"Louis, does that mean it's real?" She repeated.

Louis took a breath. "I don't know, it might be. But why does it matter? Is it because we are your friends? Exactly Luna, that word, that one word, friends. Friendship lasts forever, even in the darkest of times. A friendship can last forever, a memory never dies. We told you we were willing to risk our lives, it that risk turns into a reality, so what! We are just two people, out of six point five billion. We said we were risking our lives, if that means that we have to die, then I'm not sure about Coco, but I would be more than willing to do so. If we die Luna. That is in no way you fault. It's ours. We made that promise. Now we have to keep it." Luna took in every word like it was a glass of water.

"I need to go." Luna repeated.

"Yes. You do." Louis replied. "Remember. Five days time. Wolverine Alley. Bloodhill Manor."

Luna ran to hug him, cling onto him as hard as she could so that he couldn't vanish. But as she swung her arms, he was gone.

She sat at the kitchen table. Thinking of something to do. Until she noticed something, something odd. There was a bowl of mail in the centre of the surface, at first glance it didn't look unusual, until she realised, the bowl wasn't there when she arrived.

She took out a few letters. They were just empty envelopes! The letters weren't the problem, it was the bowl.

It was teal, with ornate designs along the rim. It didn't look even the slightest unfriendly, now that Luna studied it. But at first, it didn't seem right.

Luna decided to exit, she opened the door and attached her wings. She sighed, looking at the village emptying of people didn't look nice, even though they were unaware of what was going on, it was just the end of their day. Although one, plump woman didn't leave. She stood on the ground, staring, directly at Luna. She seemed to be wearing a police outfit. She eventually spread her wings. She flew over to the patio of which Luna was standing on.

"Name." She said.

"Erm, Luna."

"Full name."

"Luna Runder Copper."

"Age."

"Twelve."

"Occupation."

"Student."

"Right, you're coming with me."

"I'm sorry Miss, but where am I going?"

"You're coming to the council. Everyone who is found in a queeled house and is under the age of sixteen must be seen by the council to be questioned. I don't make the rules."

They wandered, silently to a large white building. The woman, who's badge said; Jill, unlocked the door and tugged Luna down a corridor and led her into a black, brick room. There were people writing on notepads, people polishing badges, and one man with a bushy brown beard, sitting at a chair in front of a table.

The woman shoved Luna into the chair next to him. stamped her foot on the floor, she saluted, and left.

"Hello." Said the man. "I am President Feather. I will be asking you some questions, and I suggest that you answer them honestly."

Luna didn't speak, she just nodded.

"Firstly, what is your *full* name?"

"Luna Runder Copper."

"Nick, please search for this name in the registrations. Secondly. What is your birth date?"

"The sixteenth of March nineteen eighty seven"

"Parents and or guardians names."

"Charlie Copper."

"Closest alliances."

"Coco Faith Wheezleberry, Louis Smith Lochsmith, Skye Minini Macdonaldson, and Anna Dreep Rigmont."

"Look for those names too, Nicholas. School?"

"Winged Beauties Boarding School for Children with the Gift."

"Lastly, your most recent location."

"1 Roasi Street."

"Thank you. Nicholas, are any of these names unregistered?" President Feather asked. Looking at an old man in a red suit looking down a list of registrations.

"Everyone here is registered Sir, except from, Luna Runder Copper." The old man replied.

"Well, seeing as your already here, you may get registered now. Kristin, take Luna to the registration association." President Feather demanded. A young woman, who only looked around twenty, accompanied Luna to a queue. On a door, of which everyone was queuing at, noted the text; AMI SALKIRE, REGISTRATION MANAGER. STRICTLY CONFIDENTIAL.

A few people entered and exited, some pleading for forgiveness, some skipping, and Luna walked in. It was a dark, navy room, with newspaper cut-outs and a desk. A desk with a tattoo pen, and some files.

Sitting on an armchair, was a woman, a skinny woman with a bony face.

"Full name and occupation." She ordered.

"Luna Runder Copper, student."

"Winged Beauties, alliances, Coco Faith Wheezleberry, Louis Smith Lochsmith, Anna Dreep Rigmont, and Skye Minini Macdonaldson. Aged twelve. Correct?" She said.

"Yes, correct." Luna answered tentatively.

The woman took Luna's shoulder and tattooed a small cross on it. It hurt dreadfully but Luna fought through it.

"Right, leave." Said the woman.

Luna left, and exited the building hurriedly. She had *almost* forgotten about the journey she was going to need to take. Until it hit her like a bullet. She had a plan.

CHAPTER THIRTEEN: BLOODHILL MANOR

Once Luna had flown all the way back to the tent, she realised that it was only Anna, James, Eve, and her.

"Where are your parents Anna?" Luna asked casually, as she arrived in the tent.

"My great grandma just had to go into hospital, she has been diagnosed with cancer and mum and dad are seeing her." Anna answered.

"Oh, sorry." Luna answered.

"No problem. No information about Skye though, just one message." Anna held up her wing;

[Anna Rigmont] Skye? Anything else?

[Skye Macdonaldson] I die on 150200.

Luna had to think quickly, but she couldn't. Somehow, something else blocked her thoughts, footage, or fantasy, she wasn't sure which... It was a blank, expressionless door, it opened at one touch, inside was a very anciently antique room, vases, and wooden tables, but there was a gloomy, filthy staircase, stone stairs, of which, Luna didn't walk, she hadn't a body, but she stridden down, it was a cellar, a dark, dead cellar, inside was Charlie, Skye, Louis, Coco, and an unfamiliar blonde girl, white-blonde she was, with big green eyes, she was crying, somehow, Luna's attention forced itself to the girl. She was wearing a rather unusual necklace, it was a dark string with only a diamond shaped ruby. She clutched it in her hands.

"Please, please I beg you, don't hurt me, don't hurt me, and don't, take my necklace, please, please I'll do anything. Anything. Please." She pleaded.

Coco and Louis were in a corner, Louis guarding Coco from any harm, Charlie was at the door, unconscious, and nose bleeding, his glasses were squint. Skye was sobbing, alone, in the middle of the floor. Still Luna's attention was on the girl. She was wearing overalls with a red and white striped top underneath. And her wavy blonde hair hung down past her shoulders. She was being clutched down by the shoulders by a cloaked figure, she sobbed deafeningly, "I'll do anything, anything, please, let me go to papa, I miss him, please, please I swear, I swear, I'll do anything. *Anything!*" Luna was striding closer...

"LUNA! WAKE UP! ARE YOU OK!" Anna was shaking her, somehow she was lying on the ground, her breathing was unsteady.

"I'm dolls rights, umm, no, alright. I'm alright." Luna answered, she was in shock.

"It's eleven thirty-three. Luna, you have to leave, Wolverine Alley, you need to leave now. Immediately." Anna reminded Luna.

Her head went straight. She put a coat on, (Louis' old one), she tiptoed out of the tent, careful not to wake Eve and James, and she stood at the edge of the cliff.

"Wait! Luna! Remember, if you go to the main centre of 'Trinit Village' then turn left, and keep walking for five minutes, then turn right, you're on Wolverine Alley." Anna said, running out of the tent. She hugged Luna.

Knowing that it may be her last chance to ever hug a friend, Luna savoured every second.

Anna hurried back into the tent, Luna walked around the broken foundations of the old cottage, and jumped. 'Trinit Village' was a small town just underneath the hill, Luna glided to the centre, which was a wishing well, and Luna, even though she didn't have a dime, wished. She wished long and hard that she wouldn't go to Bloodhill Manor to find all of her friends, dead, and this other random girl, dead, hearts frozen. That was all she wished for, everything she ever loved depended on her actions. She turned left and ran, for around five minutes, thinking about all the cruel things that may have happened by the time she arrived.

She turned round, there, right in front of her, was an old, dirty manor, she marched up the lane, and there she was, at the door, it was ajar, she pushed it further.

The lobby was exactly like her dream, there was a white vase, holding some dead peonies, and a teal teacup, with ornate designs along the rim. There was a staircase on the wall, Luna trotted down them. The walls were lit with skulls with candles in them, and the stairs were steep.

At the bottom, she reached a barred door. Indeed, Charlie was at her feet, his bloody nose dry, his glasses were now on the floor and stamped on, and his eye was bruised.

Louis and Coco were sat in a corner, clutching each other, even though they were now tied up, with Skye, and the other anonymous girl. They were tied together by a rope, and Devils held knives directly under their chins. And there he was, Barney. He was backed up with around seven, violet-eyed wolves, and he was pointing a gun, directly at Luna's face, through the bars.

"You let them go. I *demand* you let them go." Luna faltered, trying to avoid bursting into tears.

"In case you haven't noticed, *I'm* the one with the gun. Not you, you stupid girl." Barney sniggered.

"Release them Bubwul. Now." Luna threatened.

"Is that a threat? Quite pathetic, just like your idiotic little pals here, that boy, he said that *you*, were coming to get these rodents. Ha! He's just as stupid as you!" Barney answered.

"No, it's not a threat, it's only a piece of advice." Luna answered, slyly.

"Ha! Wittle baby Woona coming to save her fwiends. How cute, trust me, if I even touch this trigger, you're as dead as a doorknob." Barney said.

"LUNA RUN!" Louis yelled.

"Kill the boy." Barney demanded. The devil pressed the knife into Louis' neck, and he collapsed. Coco sobbed.

"Shut up ginger." Barney ordered. Coco fell silent.

"Let me in. At *least*." Luna ordered.

"Suit yourself." Barney answered, the door swung open and Luna entered. It then closed with a clank.

"Foitymt!" Barney yelled, the wolves charged at Luna, knocking her on the floor.

"You tell me. Die, or watch your friend's throats be sliced." Barney murmured.

Luna pretended to think, but really, she had a plan.

"Actually, Uncle B, I think, I'll do *this*!" Luna hurried up, she grabbed Barney's gun. She wasn't going to shoot him dead, just shoot his foot so that he fell down and couldn't get up. A gun trigger didn't feel right in her fingers at all, but she shot Barney's foot and he tumbled onto the floor.

"Very clever." Barney smirked.

Luna fired at all the Devils, it didn't pierce their flesh, but knocked them over. She then scrambled to the pole of which her friends were tied, and she ripped the knot. She picked up Louis by the arms, and handed him to Coco. She put him over her shoulder and ran up the staircase. Luna then untied Skye and the unknown girl with the ruby necklace. They too, scurried upstairs. Luna dropped the gun, dragged her father out of the cellar, and locked the gate. Barney shuffled to the gun, he pointed it at Luna, his finger pulled the trigger. The bullet was flying towards her, when a random man, with bright green hair, dived in front of Luna as the bullet hit him right in the chest.

Luna had never seen that man before. Ever. She didn't even know where he came from, but he had saved her life! Luna looked at his badge, it read: GERALD KIPP of LCPA. Luna was relieved but confused. She heaved her father upstairs, and found Skye chatting to the random girl, and Coco cleaning Louis' cut with a tea towel. It was of course dirty, but she was doing her best.

"Hi, you're Luna, right?" Said the random girl, "I'm Beatrice. Beatrice Natalia."

"Yeah. I'm Luna, nice to meet you Beatrice. Why were you here? I've never met you?"

"Oh, my papa saved fifty of Barney's prisoners, so he took me, as punishment for him. Papa is a Coka polisher." Beatrice answered.

Luna walked over to where Coco was sitting cross legged, beside Louis.

"How is he?" Luna asked, kneeling, and looking at the deep slash where Louis had been sliced.

"He is still breathing, and his heart is still going, but he hasn't woken up yet, and his throat is badly cut. He'll need to reattach flesh, and repair his collar bone. Besides from that, I think he's pretty." She paused, "Good."

Luna looked at her.

"Oh, shut up." Coco moaned.

"Oh, oh where am I?" Said Charlie, sitting up.

"Dad!" Luna yelled. Charlie stood up.

"Honey! But I repeat, where are we?" He answered, cuddling Luna. "And who are you?" He questioned, looking at Beatrice.

"I'm Beatrice, Beatrice Natalia."

"Pleasure, all of you, all five of you, *in*." He ordered. His wings spread so widely that there was almost an entire room in it, Beatrice, Skye, Luna, and Coco - dragging Louis in - all hopped in and got comfortable.

"OK, let's run." Said Charlie. He lifted himself off the ground, and they were off.

"What is that necklace?" Luna asked Beatrice.

"Its a Daigh stone. It only works three times, and I've used it once. It can heal any wound, but like I say, I used it once when papa lost a foot. It's very rare. And if Barney got a hold of it, he could use it to heal all of his biggest weapons, the three fire-breathing dragons. That would mean he could burn down a whole city in one blink." Beatrice replied.

"Barney has dragons? Since when were they a thing?" Luna asked.

"Oh yes. Phoenixile, Felicity, and Boggertrot. Dragons are very intelligent creatures, if you treat them nicely, giving them a good diet of dead deer and hyena, but Barney didn't, he didn't feed them at all, and now they are skinny and forced to follow orders from their commander. I know this, because I have a dragon. She is called Freya, she's a beautiful dragon, she's purple, and she can fly gorgeously. Dragons are so hard to find, they're from the middle east." Beatrice replied.

Coco wasn't listening, Luna knew this, because she was still holding the dirty cloth and dabbing Louis' wound.

"So, your saying he's abusing them?" Luna added.

"Oh yes, cruelly indeed." Beatrice sounded rather calm at the thought of three dragons imprisoned and starving to death.

"Why are you so relaxed about that?" Luna said rudely.

"Sorry to butt in." Skye started, "But dragons, they've always been treated badly. Because of their power and level of destruction. People like Pegasus's more. They look prettier. My mum has a farm, she has a herd of Pegasus's there. Well, four. Buttercup, Moonblood, Dandelion, and Stella. They're a lot of work."

"They exist too?" Luna asked stupidly.

"Of course!" Skye and Beatrice said in unison.

"Right, here is the tent. Jump out, and grab the wee lad too." Charlie ordered.

Skye hopped out first, she then helped Beatrice out, then Luna grabbed Coco's hand and heaved her out, pulling Louis out at the same time.

"Charlie Copper, pleasure to meet you." Said Charlie, wandering into the tent.

"Skye!" Anna said, cradling Skye.

Luna ran inside too, to find that the tent was getting very cramped. Inside were; Eve, who was playing with her llama; James, who was talking to Millie and Luke about Anna's gran; Anna, Skye; Beatrice, who was introducing herself to the adults; a teenage boy; and a tall, fair woman. Coco and Louis were still to come in!

Coco limped inside, holding Louis in her arms, "Blimey! What's happened to my boy? And where were you guys this whole night?" James yelled.

"We went to the bookshop, and it was shut, so we camped outside, by a sweet shop, and, yeah." Luna lied.

James nodded and laid Louis down on a blanket, sobbing. Coco kneeled down by his body.

"I've just texted papa. He's on his way." Beatrice announced to Anna, Skye, and Luna.

"Brilliant." Luna answered.

"That's my mum and Adam." Skye whispered, pointing to the woman and the teenager. Everyone nodded.

"OK, big announcement!" James yelled, wiping his eyes. "I've paid for a new cottage, in 'Trinit Village' its fully decorated too! We should leave now, it's safer in a house than a tent."

He stood up, cradling Louis like a small child, and having Eve on his back, holding her llama. Anna, Skye, and Luna stood up too, and Beatrice stood up coincidentally at the same time as Mrs Macdonaldson, Adam, Luke, and Millie. Anna grabbed Louis' bag, Luna carried Toffee, and Skye held Louis' pile of books. They trotted outside to find everyone else walking around the mountain, they jogged over and, for the first time in months, they climbed down the hill.

They came to the wishing well, and turned right. On the corner was indeed a small cottage, which looked like it had an attic and a large garden with a set of Winghinging equipment.

"Get in then!" James instructed. He again, tapped his pocket and the door unlocked. They all ran inside, the adults went and looked at the kitchen, and Beatrice, Luna, Coco, Anna, and Skye walked upstairs, Beatrice looking around, and Coco, Luna, Skye, and Anna, to see where they were going to discuss plans.

Louis' new room was lovely. It had one main bed in the middle, with teal sheets, and two sets of bunk beds for guests at the side, the flooring was dark and wooden, and there was a chest at the end of Louis' bed. In front of the two sets of bunk beds were wardrobes.

For fun, they peeked into Eve's room too, it was smaller, and had one child single, with plain, pink sheets. And because the architects knew it was a child's room, they had put three, colourful llama teddies at the top of the bed, she too, had a chest and a wardrobe. And the floor matched Louis' one.

There was also James's room, a bathroom, and a wing fitting display on the top floor.

Each one of them claimed their beds. But Beatrice was left without, so Coco and Luna agreed to top and tail.

They jogged downstairs to the new kitchen table, and Millie, Luke, Mrs Macdonaldson and Adam, were sitting eating sandwiches. James was caring for Louis in the lounge and Eve was putting all of her stuff in her room.

They all gobbled it down immediately and visited Louis directly afterwards. His neck was covered by a white bandage, and he was motionless on the furry couch.

"Perhaps he should rest upstairs. He might be safer." Beatrice said.

James agreed and he carried Louis into the bedroom, he laid him down and put the covers over him.

"Well, early night eh? You five were up late." James instructed. It was still light outside, but the most desirable thing Luna could think of was rest. They all got on bunk beds, and Coco and Luna moved pillows around to work out their top and tail arrangement.

Once everyone had started to drift off to sleep, (which was an awfully long time I must say), Beatrice bolted upwards and yelled, "I've got it!"

"Got what?" Anna and Luna said simultaneously.

"I can save him!" Beatrice took out the Daigh stone from her necklace and touched it gently to Louis' wounded throat, surely enough, to Luna's amazement, the skin re-appeared.

Each girl watched from their bunks. There was silence. No one spoke, they froze, staring at the body, it felt very tense. Until the body sat bolt upright and yelled, "River and Royal Richard!"

Everyone gasped and ran to him, they all hugged him so tightly that it was possible he may stop breathing.

"Louis, sorry to keep this short but there is something, I *need* to talk to you about, like, now." Luna asked guiltily.

"Um, sure." Louis said suspiciously. Luna helped him out into the hall, and then she asked her question.

"Louis, back at the Manor, someone saved my life. But I don't know who they are, his badge just said LCPA. Have you, read, about anything like that?"

Louis thought for a moment. "Yes actually. I read it on the blurb of that book we read at school, it said it had something to do with chapter nineteen. I can't remember what chapter your parents were on though."

They looked at each other, until there was an interruption, "Louis! You're OK!" James had waddled upstairs. Understandably, he gave him a huge hug, "You lot should be asleep though."

Everyone scurried back to their bunks. Once the lights were out, and you could only hear the mutters of the adults downstairs, there was a sudden, but quiet bang. Only Coco and Luna heard it, then suddenly, Louis' face appeared at the ladder. He whispered, "Come, I have something urgent I need to show you."

Luna and Coco got out of bed and silently followed Louis to the wing display room.

CHAPTER FOURTEEN: NO CONTACT

They all took an armchair each, and Louis handed each girl a piece of paper, "Read it. I've copied it from a book I found in our new library section."

They read through the passage;

Daily News

Archaeologist John Morris, finds a secret leading to the lair of serial killer Barney Bubwul in Pennsylvania.

Archaeologist John Morris, from London Archaeology Association, on his trip to the desert looking for ancient wing fittings, found a mysterious piece of parchment buried in the sand. After a few weeks of tests, it was discovered that the killer had planned a lair, in which he and his followers could proceed to discuss massacres. It is stood on the tallest mountain in Pennsylvania, Mount Davis. At approximately 979 metres high, we can see why this man is so hard to locate.

"I was shocked when I found out what I had found. We may be one step closer to thwarting this man." Quotes John Morris.

Any other information, please contact our service number that you will find on the back of this newspaper.

Coco grinned, Louis smiled.

"All we have to do, is go there. Then, our mission will be completed. But Pennsylvania. Jeez, that must be what? At least three and a half *thousand* miles away. But if it means we can do this. Then we're going to have to." Louis said worriedly.

"Rogererare said that we are to count up all our clues. But, do we have any?" Luna asked. "And who are River and Royal Richard?"

"We should. Oh, them, well, when I was unconscious, I spoke to them, they just told me about themselves and Barney and a weird club called LCPA, and how their family was in it. Nothing much." Louis answered. He didn't seem to have noticed what he had just said.

"Louis! Louis you're a genius! LCPA!" Luna yelped.

He looked at her, straight in the eyes, and didn't say anything, he was thinking, before he slapped his head, falling of the armchair in the act.

"I'm such an idiot! I know what it stands for! Luna, its Luna Copper Protection Agency! Well, it used to be VRPA, Vicky Runder Protection Agency, but, unfortunately, well we don't need that anymore. It runs through each, and every female in your family! To make sure, you, you, Luna, Luna, *you can't be touched.* That's why, back at Bloodhill Manor, Barney couldn't touch you! That man was there. What was his name?" Louis said.

"Gerald Kipp." Luna answered.

"Yes, that Gerald bloke. He'll be a family member or friend of one of your parents. But, don't get too happy, that is not all I found. This is from six months afterwards." He handed over two different pieces of paper and took back the old ones.

Daily News

Researcher Trevor Travelley, found the one and only lair of Barney Bubwul, criminal of murder, gun crimes, child abuse, animal abuse, and robbery.

Trevor Travelley, researcher for Sherringborr Research Team, climbed his way up Mount Davis, where the lair stood, and discovered that the structure has very many obstacles to enter, such as a maze, armed with automatic guns, a riddle, where only the correct answer can let you live, a stunt, where one must sacrifice themselves for another to enter, and a room with ivy, quick sand, a pack of comporatora wolves, and three dragons, Pheonixile, Felicity, and Boggertrot.

You must then enter the room of mysterious followers, and the criminal himself, and if you are inadequately lucky, you may live, but be imprisoned. To be the hero, you must thwart the enemy. All others, will not be seen again.

"But, what is the riddle? And, if we get it wrong, what happens?" Luna queried suspiciously.

"I don't know. But what I *do* know, now that I come to think of it, is where the LCPA headquarters is, and there are over thirty people in it. Its 27 Xnif Drive. I think, but its only visible to people who know about it. So it *will* be for us." Louis answered.

Luna wasn't expressing her true feelings. She was pretending to be interested in this riddle, when really, she was guiltily upset. There had been a *whole* association to protect her. And she hadn't once heard of it. But more importantly, her family was the one family who had that. She was lucky, and yet she hadn't known, all twelve years of her life, and she hadn't known.

Without realising, a teardrop paved its way down her face, from her eye to her chin.

Louis stood up, so did Coco. They stood in front of Luna and Louis put out his hand. He pulled her up and, hand to hand, the three of them gripped onto each other. Like they had mentally promised to do so, for as long as each one of them survived.

It was a sunny morning when they woke up. The sun shone through the gap in the curtains, filling the whole room with uplifting light. All six of them woke up to the clatter of dishes and downstairs noises.

Once they had shuffled downstairs in their pyjamas, they found Adam, Mrs Macdonalson, (otherwise known as Claire), James, Luke, Millie, Eve, Charlie, and a nice old man who was wearing an intricate golden gown, and had a very fashionable brown beard, sitting around the table.

"Papa! Where is Ma at the moment?" Beatrice yelled, running into the man's arms.

"Paris. She has promised to bring you back a macaron." Answered the man.

"Mail!" James yelled, as a khink, (group of such creatures), or winglets flew through the window, dropped several letters onto the table, and flew away, "And the pets are arriving in half an hour."

"Luke, there's one for you. Claire, there you go, Louis, hmm, who have you been talking to? And one, ooh, one, one is addressed to, 'Luna Copper, Coco Wheezleberry, and Louis Lochsmith'. Very formal. Oh! One for myself!"

Luna, Coco, and Louis exchanged looks. They took the letter and opened it. The writing was printed by a computer, (or in this case, a Roxo, which is a computer, that floats on two keys, A, and L, which sprout gliders).

Dear Luna Copper

    Coco Wheezleberry

    Louis Lochsmith

Hi! Did you hear, did you hear! Sorry, our dad wrote the names. He's sooo posh. Its River here. Royal is in the garden with Mist. He's our dog. He can't fly. Sorry, I'm going off on a tangent here. Royal told me exactly what to tell you three, so I'm going to.

Sorry, I'm Royal, I'm here to actually tell you what you need to know. We are twins, I'm the smart one, don't tell River. We want to help you. This is for Luna, this next paragraph. We met your Mum. She's our second cousin once removed. You're our second cousin twice removed. We know your trying to kill Barney Bubwul, and we know how. We just need a way to meet you.

Coco, this sounds crazy, but your house burning was all over the papers. We read all about you. And your siblings. They should be safe. They didn't arrive when you expected them to, because we helped them, we explained everything, and they are safe and sound.

Louis, River, well, she has this book about tragic accidents, and your one was chapter four, I remember this, because River is always talking about you. I think she sort of likes you a little bit. But that's beside the point. Your cleverness will come in handy.

We are going on a train tomorrow. We are going to camp on the mountain behind your stay. And we were wondering if we could meet you, all three of you, on the mountain. Alone though, there is more we need to discuss.

Yours truly,

River, and Royal Richard

It took a while to persuade the adults to approve of the three of them to leave the house alone, seeing as there were Devils on patrol. But they eventually approved if all six of them went together, Luna, Coco, Louis, Beatrice, Anna, and Skye.

"Who is that letter from anyway?" Coco asked intriguingly.

"Nobody. A scam, probably." Louis replied, tucking the letter in his pocket.

"Then why are you keeping it?" Luna asked rudely.

"Because. It might not be a scam, I've got nothing to hide." Louis answered.

"Read it out loud then. Go on, go on." Coco asked daringly.

"No."

Luna and Coco smirked at each other.

"You really are a bad liar." Coco said meanly.

"Oi! I'm not lying! I just, keep things, personal." He answered.

Luna shrugged, "Suit yourself."

Louis nodded and they trotted upstairs. Beatrice had packed a small bag, which she had kept folded up in her overall pocket in the cellar, with a small supply of clothes, two books for pure enjoyment, and one stuffed pillow of the Mona Lisa. It was at the bottom of her, very, made bed.

Anna had packed a large gym bag, full of clothing, makeup, wing paint, a hairbrush, a toothbrush, a pillow designed with the pop band Ce'Rovi, and a notebook. Her bed was very clean and very made too.

Skye had nothing but a ring, kept in a box, and a bottle of water. Which were both messily scattered all over her bunk, and her sheets were hanging off the side.

Coco only had one book, which was small, and written by a fictional author, Shawn McDae.

Luna just had her old jewellery box from her mother, and Toffee. And she had propped up her pillow.

Louis had packed a whole rucksack and still hadn't unpacked. Apart from the mismatched items, the room was in good condition, Louis put the envelope under his pillow, and sat on his bed with The Tales Of Tamara And Ti'. Coco and Luna climbed up to their bunk and Coco picked up a book too, and Luna decided to just lie down.

As she lay there, she envisioned an image. She was standing on a cracked rock. Just her. She was alone, somehow she was carrying another rock, it was a very peaceful forest, the trees were as green as the moss on the rock, she was in the quiet, she hadn't had that before. There was a river, it was still, the birds choruses increased the relaxation of the scenario and the fish blew bubbles up to the surface of the water. It was calm, it felt like it was the last time to be calm. Her breathing was steady, her heart was no longer pounding with anxiety, she was okay, she was alive, and isn't that, the most important thing of all.

She awoke to a shock, Louis and Coco were sitting in front of her, staring at her.

"What?" She asked confusedly.

"Luna, are you okay?" Coco asked anxiously.

"Yes, I'm fine. Why?"

Louis joined in, "Luna, you, you fell asleep, but, you didn't just sleep, you talked, weirdly though, like, just, you mixed together a few letters and said them, but the main ones were sch, and dreque. It means nothing though, I looked it up."

Beatrice had hurried upstairs, she was carrying a large book. Even with three friendly greetings, she hurried up to her bunk, opened the book, slammed it down, and read. Her eyes scanned through it like they were robotic.

"Pack up though, Beatrice, fetch Anna and Skye... actually I'll do it then." Louis said, he hurried downstairs. Once the room door had closed, Coco jumped down from her bed and grabbed the letter from underneath Louis' pillow.

"Coco! You really shouldn't be looking at that! It's private!" Luna said responsibly.

"Argh never mind that, I'ts from, I'ts from, Rory Smith." Coco sniggered, "Come on, don't be a goody two shoes."

Luna shuffled over.

To Louis,

Yes, I'm fine thank you, the school work I've got is so much harder than that. We have to label sixty wing fittings to the correct owner, and get the accuracy level at exactly 75%. Or else we get three hours of lectures with the Head. Oh, how I wish I went to Winged Beauties. Uniquae is so intimidatingly boring, we have to speak Dropendeque constantly, and it's so tricky to pronounce a normal conversation! For example;

Hello – Aghallda

How are you – Friopt Junapraeque

I'm good – Shoomerd Drecoper

I'm bad – Shoomerd Stidell

I'm okay – Shoomerd Uniprae

Goodbye – Xuinfra

I know right! That's just an everyday chat! Ugh! We even have extra lessons on it! But saying complicated words like psychological! My gosh! Its Drequatradecropasa! For psychological! Dropendeque is in the top three most complicated languages in history, but according to my head teacher, 'you need to learn what you need to learn.'

How are you anyway? And are you actually friends with Coco Wheezleberry? My brother Archi is obsessed with that story. On your last letter you said you wanted me to teach you Dropendeque. Well, I sort of just did, but you wanted to know the seasons;

Summer – Stropegequa

Winter – Wadergatra

Spring – Streque

Autumn – Ausumbrae

And you wanted to know the numbers to ten;

Proque

Trumbag

Yergep

Frouque

Fivvequa

Serpentag

Froppequa

Eeque

Drukk

Trenze

There you go. You won't remember that though will you. Anyways. Good day.

Rory Smith

"I hope you found what you were looking for." Said Louis, entering the room.

"Louis! It was her." Said the two girls in shock, pointing at each other.

"Liar!" Luna yelled.

"Tell tale." Coco answered back.

"Well, I suppose I can't trust either of you now. That was a private letter from Rory! And for your information! Before you start thinking up things like she's my girlfriend or something, she's my cousin! Rory, *Smith*. Louis *Smith* Lochsmith. I can't believe you! I let you into my home to take shelter from the killers and this is how you repay me! By snooping through my private letters? What a horrible thing to do!" He yelled angrily, snatching the letter and slamming the door shut.

Anna and Skye stood rooted to the spot, silent.

"I can't believe you talked me into this! It *is* a horrible thing to do! Look at how upset he is now!" Luna sobbed.

She too, climbed down the ladder, barged past Anna and Skye, and left the room. She scurried downstairs to the living room, where she found Louis on the couch, polishing his wings.

Luna turned round, "No no, don't leave, my Valentine's cards are here, if you want to look at them too!" Louis yelled. Luna exited. She found her dad drinking a beer at the table and went over to him.

"Oh dad, Louis is angry at me and so is Coco! They're the only friends I've ever had and now its ruined!" She sobbed.

"Oh Luna, it's not ruined, you know, me and my mate Peter Leon, we had about three fights a week, we are still friends thirty three years later. It'll be okay. Here, have a biscuit." He replied, handing Luna a gingersnap.

Luna nibbled at it cautiously.

"Talk to them. For whatever you've done just apologise." Charlie advised. Luna nodded.

She entered the living room, "Louis I'm sorry. I shouldn't have looked at that. You're right. It's horrible. Are we good?" She was, not, a good pep talker.

"It's just, Rory. She is really nice, but all her friends have shut her out for some reason, I just try to keep her happy. We're good. I just wish you hadn't read that. I've packed up for tomorrow. Tell Coco and everyone to pack up too. We're leaving early." He answered. Luna nodded.

She entered the bedroom, and Beatrice was reading a newspaper, Coco was reading, Anna was unpacking a few items, and Skye was making her bed.

Coco looked up, and once she had realised it was Luna, she hung her head disappointingly.

"Ugh, why is she here." Anna said meanly.

Skye looked at Luna with a bored expression,

"Because I have nowhere else to. You guys better pack up, were leaving early doors."

"No." Coco answered, not lifting her head.

"What do you mean 'no'?"

"I mean no. I won't go thank you, I'll stay here and not get my heart shot by a bullet because *somebody* took the wrong path. But, if you're such an idiot to do so, then go ahead."

Luna was temporarily visited with the urge to punch Coco in the face.

"I'll go. I like a bit of excitement." Beatrice said kindly.

"Thank you Beatrice." Luna said.

Anna and Skye weren't talking.

"What have I done to you? You're the one who *insisted* we read the letter." Luna said furiously.

"Well you blamed it on me! You looked too!" Coco yelled.

"Oh really! *I'm* the idiot! Sure. Live in your little fantasy where absolutely nothing you do is wrong. Duh! My bad, no! You're the bad guy here." Luna screamed.

"You just shut up." Coco demanded, she slammed her book shut and jumped down. "I'm not in the wrong here! And if you want to go get your ugly head cut off by Barney's knife then go on. And who cares who these stupid Richards are anyway! Their just some random people who like us."

"They're family! If you *had* one you'd understand!" Luna knew she shouldn't have said that. Cocos eyes watered, she turned bright red. Her hands clenched, without thinking, she punched Luna right in the nose.

"No one. And I mean no one, insults my family." She threatened, running out of the room and into the wing display.

Luna knew her nose was bleeding, she touched it gently, and her finger came back painted scarlet. Luna fell back into the corner. She was dizzy. All she remembered was Anna shouting on James, and Charlie, and Skye breathing heavily. Then someone entered, yelling, "What happened to my daughter! Luna, Luna are you alright?" Luna tried to answer, but as she opened her mouth to speak blood filled it. Then there were people in white, who flew in through some gap, and they put her on a bed, then she was on the move. They took her to a big white building, with the Emergency sign then she was still, they were checking something on her body, then it was just a big white blur for around three hours."

CHAPTER FIFTEEN: THE THREE Rs

Luna awoke to a shock, she was on a hospital bed. There were people talking outside, she could just hear them.

"Is she OK? Please Doctor, Christopher, please, is she alright?" Said a man.

"She seems to be OK sir. Please calm down. Although when the paramedics arrived with her she had lost a lot of blood. Any bacteria could have entered the wound. Further studies on the mark prove that the punch was by an Octrum Glove, which you will know can cause up to twenty-five times the injury as an ordinary one. We do not know who injured your daughter though sir. We need to directly ask the patient who was in the room at the time, and what she can remember from that time. An Octrum injury can cause memory loss. We need to do further tests as well. We will also need your phone number and your address." Said an unfamiliar voice.

"Oh, thank you Doctor. Thank you." Said the man.

"Any time. Visiting time is over though Sir. We will open again at nine o'clock tomorrow morning." The so called Doctor announced.

"OK. Thank you. Come on everyone." Said the man.

There was a series of footsteps and then the Doctor opened the curtains and entered.

"Oh, hello honey. Are you OK if I ask you some questions?" He asked kindly.

"Um, yes." Luna mouthed.

"OK. Firstly. What is your birthday sweetie?"

"Umm, the, the sixth. No, the sixteenth of, of, *March*? Yes, March. Nineteen eighty seven. I think."

"Thank you. Secondly, I need you to be honest. Who was with you when you were hit?"

"Umm, I think, it was, Coco? I think she was there. Beatrice was there. Anna. I think, yeah. And Skye. Yeah. That's all."

"Do you know their last names hon?"

"Coco, Wheezle, berry? Yeah. Beatrice Natalia. Anna, umm, Anna… Anna Rigmont, that's it. And, Skye, Macdonaldson."

"OK. You're doing very well, now this is the question that you have to answer honestly. Please Miss Copper, this is vital information. What can you remember from that time?"

Luna thought, "I, I walked in. And, no one but Beatrice was happy with me. Then, I can't remember who. But someone jumped down the bunk bed. Then, then they shouted at me, and they, they, I don't know what they did."

"Two things. Firstly, you said jumped *down*. Is it bunks?" Doctor Christopher said. Luna nodded unsurely. "OK. Who is on the bottom bunks?"

"Er, Beatrice, and, and Anna." Luna answered.

"OK. So that means it Would have been either Coco, or Skye. Secondly, why were they angry at you?"

"Er, I, I blamed Coco for something."

"So, was it Coco? If you can't remember who it was, that's OK."

Luna thought, she tried to remember, but she couldn't. "I don't know, I'm sorry Doctor."

"That's ok. You rest darling, you need sleep. Feel free to eat something, just ring the bells." He pointed to a series of bells hung by string, each noting a type of service;

There was 'Cook', 'Doctor', 'Entertainment', and 'Questions'.

The doctor exited, and Luna laid on her side, her long, silky black hair giving her extra comfort, fiddling with her thoughts. She had so many questions, that her mind drew a list of all of them;

- *What was an Octrum Glove*
- *Who hit her (at the back of her head)*
- *Who was the man talking to Doctor Christopher*

- *What was her injury*

- *Why was she connected to a heartbeat monitor*

She was wildly confused, and she just sat there, thinking.

As she awoke, she looked at the small, analogue clock flying in front of her, it noted '08:56'. It was early for her, but somehow it seemed right. She sat up, and found a gift, it was Glee! With a letter.

Luna opened the letter;

Dearest Luna,

Thank you for lending me Glee. He is a very good mail carrier. All students have gotten their pets back now. I see you have gotten a small injury. How did this happen? Please don't feel forced to reply to me. I'm just an old man writing to children. Homework and exam results are being sent home as well, you may find yours under your cage.

Yours sincerely,

Arthur Borwung Whiteshield Rogererare

Luna got rarely excited about school things, although now she couldn't be more excited to see her results. They were confusing.

Wing Painting: U

Wingcare and Maintenance: A

Winghinging: R

Wing Picking: RC

Flying: H

She was dearly confused. But, before she could think properly, a crowd of chattering people entered her cubicle. Louis, looking pale, and holding

Coco's hand; an unfamiliar girl with long brown hair and blue eyes; two dark haired people, around Luna's age, also holding hands; James, carrying Eve and a cage with a small dog in it; Mr Natalia and Claire, holding Skye and Adams hands; Beatrice carrying a small red bag; Millie, holding Anna, Luke, and Charlie, wearing brand new glasses.

Eve dropped a self-made card onto Lunas bed, it had a crayoned pink flower on it, and the words 'GET WEL SOON'. Drawn on in blue. She opened it up; 'TO LUNA GET WEL SOON LOVE FROM EVE'. Luna thanked her and James stroked her hair. Anna and Skye gave her a box of white chocolates in the shapes of Winglets, hugged her, and hurried out with Claire, Adam, Millie, and Luke.

Beatrice sat down, and her father left. Charlie sat on her bed and kissed her on the head, he then said, "Oh hon, someone's really hit the jackpot this time huh. I hope you're alright."

"I'm fine Dad. Really, I'm just dizzy." Luna reassured her father. He nodded, gave her another kiss, and exited.

"Rory, Rory Smith." Said the blue-eyed girl. She was wearing a dark green suit with boots buckled by golden metal, and a badge with the letter U on it. She reached out her gloved hand and shook Lunas. "I'm not here to mess around. I'm here to win. Win the war. Good versus Evil."

"Pleasure?" Luna answered wisely.

"I'm River. I'm a twin. I wrote to you, you seem nice. Are you OK? You don't look it. Do you need anything?" Said the other girl, the boy holding her hand shoved a piece of gum in her mouth to stop her talking.

"I'm Royal. We want to help you guys. We know where the battleground is, and how to get there. We just need your trust." Said the boy.

"Sure. Thanks. It's good to meet you all." Luna answered professionally.

"Do you want a piece of toast?" Said Beatrice irrelevantly.

"Yeah sure. Thanks Beatrice."

Beatrice took out a plate from an unknown oasis and handed it to Luna politely. As expected, there was a slice of buttered toast on it. Luna nibbled awkwardly.

It was only now that Luna noticed a small, what looked like, dragon, circling Rory's feet.

"Ah, don't worry. Everyone at Uniquae has a dragon. This is Alexander. He's not hostile... yet." She said.

Louis and Coco stepped forwards. "Are you OK? Really Luna. Are you?" Louis said worryingly.

"I'm fine thanks." Luna said uncomfortably.

"Do you, remember, anything, from, last night?" Coco asked, shifting her weight from one foot to the other.

"Not really." Luna answered truthfully.

Coco didn't look happy. Not at all, Luna didn't know why.

"It's OK." Louis said, as Coco panicked, "We need to go somewhere."

Luna shrugged and nodded, they left.

"Luna," Beatrice started, "Luna I know what happened last night. I, I don't know if I should say though."

"No. Don't. I think Skye or Coco should say themselves." Luna answered specifically.

"Mm." Beatrice said, without saying anything, she left.

"I'd better get back to Uniqae. We leave tomorrow. Eleven o'clock. I'll tell, everyone." Rory said. She too, exited.

"I'm getting hungry now. Let's go to the kitchens, now. Royal!" River said demandingly. She ran off.

As Royal turned his back to leave, Luna interrupted, "Er, Royal, can you tell me what these grades are please?"

"Sure."

"U, A, R, RC, and H."

"U is Unbelievable. A, is Alright. R is Remarkable, RC is Rememberable Choices, and H is Horrid. Why?" He answered cleverly.

"Thank you. No, no. I'm just wondering." She answered untruthfully.

Royal exited and Luna picked up a different newspaper from the small wooden desk beside her bed. The newspaper didn't include anything interesting, and where it mentioned Winghinging, someone had spilt coffee right over the main paragraph.

She turned it over, and discovered one headline that seemed the slightest bit interesting; 'UNUSUAL YOPPIR FOUND IN FAMOUS WINGHINGING PLAYER'.

Luna read;

Jim Scott, Australian Eagles Hitter, was being questioned by a young boy named Elliot Pice. The boy asked him an unusual question, what is his Yoppir? A Yoppir, as many know, is an animal unique to one's mind, when they are in danger or about to be killed, the Yoppir appears in the persons mind. A Yoppir is an animal, dependant on the persons personality. It only appears in the mind. Everyone has a Yoppir and sees it at least once before they die. Or before danger strikes. The player then answered 'Well, it's unusual, but my Yoppir is a coyote. I've only seen him once. Before I broke my leg.' The coyote is not a common Yoppir. But that was not the only mysterious piece of his text. When he said the gender of the coyote, it confused many, because a Yoppir is never known as female or male. It is only an animal. The young boy then asked what it looks like when you see a Yoppir. The player replied, "Well, it appears white. Bright, and white. It just appears as a big white silhouette. Then it fades away.' To read more about Yoppirs, please visit our website to buy our recommended books.

Luna wanted to know about these so called Yoppirs, so she rang her 'Entertainment' bell. In around thirty seconds a man with combed hair and a moustache stood straight at her curtain.

"Would ze girl like books or ze television?" He said fancily.

"Books please, anything on Yoppirs." Luna replied.

The man walked out, his carefully polished shoes clattering on the floor. He then returned with two large volumes. 'What Are Yoppirs? – A Timothy McLaughlin Production'. And, 'What Does My Yoppir Mean? – A Timothy McLaughlin Production'.

Luna thanked the man and took both of the books. She already knew what a Yoppir was, so she opened the other one.

'*Chapter One – What are the most common Yoppirs*

The most common Yoppir is a sloth. With over two million appearances. Although it isn't the only popular one. This is the top ten.

1. *Sloth – Signs of a laid back person*
2. *Bear – Signs of someone who feels safe most of the time*
3. *Elephant – Signs of wisdom and loyalty*
4. *Scottish Terrier – Signs of an independent person*
5. *Horse – Signs of a person overwhelmed with freedom*
6. *Owl – Signs of a personally silent person*
7. *Giraffe – Signs of uniqueness and pride in a person*
8. *Kitten – Signs of an innocent and curious person*
9. *Pig – Signs of a lucky person*
10. *Sheep – Signs of someone who knows their place*

These are the rarest of Yoppirs, top ten:

1. *Dove – Signs of hope*
2. *Parrot – Signs of truth and calmness to the fall of humanity*
3. *Wolf – Signs of leadership and bravery*
4. *Tiger – Signs of courage*
5. *Otter – Signs of kindness, friendship, and peace in a person*
6. *Butterfly – Signs of transformation and spiritual rebirth in a person*
7. *Foe – Signs of bitterness and hatred towards any enemy in a person*
8. *Dragon – Signs of unhidden knowledge and strength in a person*
9. *Unicorn – Signs of diversity and positivity in a person*
10. *Coyote – Signs of a trickster and smuggler*

Want to find out what your Yoppir is? Put yourself in the smallest danger possible. Then read your paragraph in Chapter Two to discover exactly what it means. Remember, a Yoppir only appears when it feels it needs to.'

Luna placed the book down on her bedsheets. Then Coco and Louis entered.

"Luna. I'm so sorry." Coco began. Luna looked up.

CHAPTER SIXTEEN: PENNSYLVANIA

"So, you're telling me, you stole an Octrum glove from the cupboard. You then tried it on, not knowing what it did. Then you *forgot* you were wearing it and punched me in the face with it on, not knowing it done twenty-five the damage! I had a concussion!" Luna yelled after listening to Coco's story.

"I told you. I'm sorry." Coco replied miserably.

"I don't want to hear it. You know why? You gave me a head injury, and you didn't even know you were doing it! I'm now stuck in this *stupid* hospital because you injured me. You really did. Not only physically. I feel like you've pulled my heart out and stamped on it. You were meant to be my friend. My best friend." Luna replied.

"It's not Coco's fault." Louis started.

"Oh, so now you're on her side." Luna said moodily.

"I'm not taking anyone's side Luna." He sounded angry. He gripped Coco's wrist.

"*Louis!*" Luna almost felt like she wanted to forget all about both of them.

"Luna. Calm down and let me speak." Louis said angrily.

"Fine. Speak."

"I wasn't asking for permission."

"JUST SPEAK!!!" Luna knew she was going too far. But she wasn't bothered.

"You insulted Coco. You said she had no family. You didn't think you did before you met your dad. You thought he was *dead.* Well Coco thinks that too. But she has more family than you. She has three siblings and you just have your dad."

"Oh, so *I'm* the one who's being insulting."

"I'm just stating the truth. I'm only trying to say that you owe Coco an apology. But she owes you one too." Louis sounded calmer.

"Fine. I'm sorry." Luna said angrily.

"You have to *mean* an apology."

Luna took a deep breath, "Coco, I'm sorry."

Coco smiled, "I'm sorry too."

Luna stood up and Coco wrapped her arms around her neck. Luna did the same. Simultaneously, they reached out matching arms for Louis to join in the hug.

"That's my two friends again." He said, grinning. He too, joined in the hug.

"Too sentimental. Pack up. Change of plan. We're leaving in an hour. With, or without you." They didn't need three guesses to figure out who was speaking, Rory had entered. Alexander was perched on her shoulder. She was out of her suit. She was wearing a navy blue polo shirt and a navy pair of trousers. Her boots were still on though. And her hair was in a high ponytail tied by a navy ribbon.

Beatrice arrived with the twins. She was still carrying her red bag and had changed into her usual overalls and red t-shirt. Her beautiful blonde hair was in pigtails and her large green eyes glittered.

Royal was in denim trousers and a white shirt. River was wearing a long white skirt and had a denim top on. They looked quite the pair. On Royals back was a brown backpack.

The trio exited their hug, Louis had left his bag outside so he went and grabbed it. Once he had entered again Rory had picked up her *navy* handbag.

"What about Skye and Anna?" Luna asked worriedly.

"Oh them. They went off to do some sort of horseback retreat. Their fine." Louis replied.

"We've got two bottles of water and some food. Also, a blanket in case we get stuck in the middle of some kind of room. What about everyone else." Royal explained.

"I've got an extra ribbon, water, food, a notebook, a quill and ink, and lipstick." Rory answered.

"Why have you got *lipstick*?" Louis asked.

"Hey! You never know this guy's standards."

Louis rolled his eyes. "I've packed for me, Coco, and Luna. So I've got three waters, some sandwiches, three pillows. Once again in case we get stuck or need to sit down. I have a compass, some changes of clothes, a hairbrush for the ladies. Oh and a few packets of crisps."

"I've packed ten pounds, a water bottle, and a carrot." Beatrice said.

"A carrot?" Coco asked rudely.

"Yes." Beatrice answered.

Coco nodded.

"We leave in forty-five minutes. Anyone got anything to pass the time?" Rory said.

"Umm. Oh! What are all your Yoppirs? I'll look them up." Luna said. It was the only way to avoid something stupid like I Spy or Truth or Dare or What I Did Today.

"Mine is a dragon." Said Louis.

"How did you find that out?"

"It really doesn't matter. Just look it up!"

Luna read the dragon paragraph.

"*A dragon Yoppir is a Yoppir that shows cleverness. If you're Yoppir is a dragon you are smart and powerful because of it. You don't stop trying. And if nothing works, you force it to.*" Luna read.

Louis nodded.

"I'm a unicorn." Coco said.

Luna read, "*A unicorn Yoppir is a Yoppir that proves you're a humorous person and bring joyful vibes to everyone around you. You're not only funny, but positive and always think of the good things.*"

Coco grinned with pride.

"My Yoppir is a giraffe." Beatrice added solemnly.

"*A giraffe Yoppir is one that shows you're a unique person in an awesome way. You're your own person but don't care one dime. You're almost like a mouse to an elephant. You always win.*" Luna read.

"Mine's a horse." River said.

Luna read, "*A horse Yoppir shows you are free to ride on your own steeds, you do what you feel like when you feel like doing it, and you don't let anyone or anything stop you.*"

"Mine is an otter." Royal said soothingly. To Luna his voice sounded soothing and calm.

"*A horse Yoppir proves that you are a friendly and calming person. Friendship and love comes first to you and you stand strong and proud with this point. You are usually clever and use this to help others.*"

"That does sound like me." He spoke. Looking straight at Luna and grinning. She smiled back.

"My Yoppir is a sheep." Rory added.

"*A sheep Yoppir*' is~"

"I don't need it looked up. I know what it is. Ten minutes. Luna, change. And *do your hair!*" Rory shouted, she ordered everyone out as Luna changed into her green t-shirt and black trousers. She shoved her silky black hair into a ponytail and swung it to the right.

"Everyone ready?" Rory queried.

"Yeah!" Yelled River, Royal, Louis, Coco, Beatrice, and Luna in unison.

"To Pennsylvania!" Coco yelled.

"To Pennsylvania!" Everyone else called back.

Coco's enchanted wing paint helped a lot. She held Louis' hand, who held Rive'rs, who held Royal's, who held Luna's, who held Rory's, who held Beatrice's, who kept the glide.

It took about three hours with Coco's speed. It was major jetlag for Luna once they had arrived. Newcastle time it was eleven am. In Pennsylvania however, it was five am. It was still dark.

They all gasped with relief as they landed on the rocks.

Louis sat on a rock, Luna and Coco sat on either side of him. Beatrice sat crossed legged, trying to make a fire, with only two sticks, one flame appeared and went out again. Rory sat down on a log. The twins hugged each other as their teeth clattered.

"You do realise Alexander can start a real fire Belle." Rory said rudely.

"Beatrice, and please." Beatrice answered.

The tiny dragon inhaled deeply then exhaled an entire camp fire. They all sat around it until they all fell asleep. (Fortunately, nobody rolled into the fire in the night).

The sun shone like a lantern in the morning. It woke everyone up at around the same time.

"Oi!" Coco yelled.

"What." Said everyone else, either stretching or waking up.

"I know we're here to like kill the killer and stuff, but in case no one has noticed, were in the USA!" Coco screamed.

"Oh yeah!" Yelled everyone.

First of all, they went to a fun fair, and each of them got 'cotton candy' – basically, candy floss.

"Cotton candy? Jee. Being American is weird." Coco said stupidly.

"For the last time, Coco. You're not American. Your just here on a holiday." Louis answered, rolling his eyes.

"Look everyone, ice cream, Beatrice, what about that ten pounds? It's one dollar. Dollar! Oh my god! For one ice cream? And there's seven of us." Coco said, munching her 'cotton candy'.

"Seven strawberry ice creams please." Said Luna, the others trailing behind her.

"You lot English?" Said the man at the stall.

"Newcastle." They all said in unison.

The man shook his head. "Right, money."

Luna handed over the seven pounds.

"You serious?" Said the man at the stall. His badge said Bill. He really liked money.

"Of course I am." Luna answered.

"What is this? Game money?"

"No. It's pounds."

"*Pounds?* Nah, I need, *dollars.*"

"Oh sugar. Currencies." Louis whispered to the others. "Thank you. Sorry for wasting your time Bill." They walked away.

Next, they looked around a bookshop, all they got was a five dollar discount coupon for quilt covers -when they had no bed. They found it on the floor.

They then scanned their eyes over a sweet shop window.

Then they found themselves running down a filthy alley after hearing a gunshot. That, was not something they were used to hearing.

They next of all they looked in a bakery, there was a kind old lady behind the till. She was selling something called, 'key lime pie'. This got rather confusing to all the British people, there was no sign of lime anywhere!

"Hmm. Quilt covers, no bed, cotton candy, dollars, key lime pie. Honestly!" Coco yelled confusedly.

"That was fun. Although why on earth is no one panicking about that serial killer in the field! Running about with a gun and no one moves a muscle!" River complained.

"Right, let's get up that mountain." Said Rory. Everyone burst out laughing.

"Huh? How on Saturn is that funny?"

"Umm, you've, you've got a little something." Coco snorted, pointing to her lip.

Rory wiped it off. She had a big moustache of 'cotton candy' stuck on her face.

Once everyone had gotten their acts straight. They got into pairs as planned, well, one solo. River and Royal – River held their bag, and held onto Royals leg, and Royal flew. Coco and Louis – Coco held the bag, and held onto Louis' leg, and Louis flew. Beatrice and Rory – Beatrice held both bags, and kept Alexander hidden from sight of a non-flier. And held Rory's leg, and Rory flew. Luna flew by herself.

"When I say go, we all, do our ups. Three!" Everyone got into launch position.

"Two!" Everyone focused.

"One!" They lifted up.

"GO!" Rory yelled, they took off.

CHAPTER SEVENTEEN: THE ONE GOODBYE THAT RIPS YOUR HEART FOREVER

They reached the top of the mountain. There was a building there. It looked like a house. But broken. Very, broken. The door was ajar. One push, it opened. The interior was no nicer, it was a living room. Although nothing in there lived, there was a dead rat at the doorway and the couch was spewing stuffing. The floorboards were cracked or out of place.

The kitchen was no better. All of them stuck together. In the kitchen there was a small vent. It was obvious that they had to go in. Royal went first. Then Louis, then Coco, then Beatrice, then River, then Rory, then Luna shoved all the bags in, she picked up the dragon, and hopped in. It was very tight. There was rotten fruit all around, you'd never know when your knee would crack an ancient egg. The cobwebs made it even more disgusting.

They jumped down to the new room. It was filthy, grey, and blood dripped from the roof occasionally. It was spacious though. Coco sat in a corner. She started breathing heavily.

"Coco. Coco you're OK." Louis said, bending down to Coco's height.

"No. No. No. No. No. The. The unicorn. It's here." She spoke. She screamed, her head in her hands.

"Coco. Calm down." Louis said, tucking her hair behind her ears.

He was covered in rotten egg, and he had a dead spider in his hair. But Coco stopped screaming.

He handed her a bottle of water and she took a sip. She smiled. Louis nodded.

Coco stood up. They looked around. There was nothing there except from a few rotten pieces of fruit and cobwebs.

"We can set up camp here. We'll sleep, then continue." Louis said cleverly.

He opened up his bag and took out three pillows. He took the middle. Coco sat next to him. She held his arm for safety. She had seen her Yoppir. You can't blame her.

Luna didn't sit down. She checked the walls. The roof, the floor. Nothing. It might take a while to open. She thought. She was right.

Luna awoke before everyone else. She was dreaming, and a bright, white wolf silhouette appeared. She yelled as it appeared. It awoke everyone else.

"Luna?" Said Royal. Standing up.

"I'm fine. Although, I saw my Yoppir." She answered.

"What is it?" Louis asked.

"A wolf. It means leadership and bravery."

Louis hugged her.

"Guys. There's a ladder. It leads through the ceiling." Beatrice said.

"Pick up your bags. We're going up." Rory ordered. Louis repacked and so did everyone else. River jumped up the ladder and they all followed, carrying their bags. They climbed all the way up then reached a jump, over ivy, and onto a metal platform. As each and every one of them jumped down, the clatter echoed around the room.

Once they had all gotten down safely they realised that it was the maze, one wrong turn then they were dead.

"Always turn left?" Coco said unsurely.

"Worth a shot." Louis answered. It seemed to be working. Until they reached a guessing corner, where you couldn't go left. Or right. You could only go through one of the three corridors. They tried the left one. And jumped back immediately as the bullets demolished the wall and set it alight. They tried the right one. It was correct. They kept going left then they turned right, they could see the ladder. They held each other's hands tight. They knew what they were going to do. They ran, a bullet shot but only shot Louis' bag. The water leaked out of the bag but they jumped onto the ladder and climbed it quickly.

They jumped down to another empty but filthy room. It had nothing but a red button. They let go of each other. And Louis hit the button.

"Welcome. Your riddle awaits. Are you ready for the decision of your life." Said a eery female voice.

Without an answer she continued.

"I have white skin, thirteen hearts, no other organs, and I am ruled by the king and queen. What am I? You have one guess each."

"An octopus." Yelled River.

"No. An octopus has three hearts."

"You!" Coco yelped, she wasted her guess trying to humiliate the voice.

"No. I have zero hearts."

"The sphinx." Luna guessed. Trying to be clever but only guessing.

"No. Nobody knows how many hearts she has."

Louis stepped forward. "Ha! That's easy. Watch and learn. A deck of cards. Now let us through."

There was an ominous silence.

"Your wish is my command."

Everyone gasped. A ladder was thrown down. Everyone climbed up again.

It was an understatement to call it a task. It was a tiny box room. With a door and a Devil.

As they entered, the Devil spoke.

"Let us take one of you to the torture chamber, we might just let you in. If you allow us to take one, maybe one twin."

Louis charged towards the Devil. "You're not taking anyone. You useless, stupid, evil, beast."

"I'll go." River said sadly.

"No." Louis answered, without looking round.

"Yes. You lot don't like me that much do you. I'm too hyper. Too upbeat. There are children out there Louis, hear them cry. People are dying Louis, I can't let them die."

"But you're too young."

"Age doesn't matter. It's about how you spend those years, and I've spent them with the best of people."

River shook off Royal's clutch. She walked up to the Devil. "Take me."

"You can't go." Louis pleaded.

"Why?"

Louis sobbed.

"I love you."

River walked back to Louis, she whispered in his ear, she hugged him. Left him standing there, she walked towards the Devil. Royal ran towards the Devil.

"YOU BRING HER BACK. YOU BRING HER BACK." He yelled. He fell to his knees.

There was a clatter of an elevator and then a deafening scream. Louis stood there. He turned round and walked back to the girls, wiping his face.

"Right. Let's wait for that Devil." He said.

"Its OK to be sad." Coco said. Rubbing his arm. He shook her hand off.

"Its fine. She was irritating. Annoying. Weird. Hyper. Its him you should be worrying about." He pointed to Royal, who was on his knees. Banging on the floor. He was crying. He was in pain. Physical pain. Twin telepathy.

Luna walked up to him. "She's gone Royal. I'm so, so sorry."

Royal nodded solemnly. The Devil returned. He had bloodstains on his cloak. "You may enter the quick room."

Louis, Royal, Luna, Coco, Rory, and Beatrice entered. It was quicksand, all across the floor, the walls were smothered in ivy, a pack of wolves were spread across the room, staring at them menacingly. And there was three, bony dragons with golden chains with golden letters attached. One had a P. One had an F. One had a B.

"One word." Louis began. "Run." He shot across the sand, jumping over jump ropes of ivy, and limbo-ing under shots of fire. He jumped on the back of a flying wolf and jumped onto the platform. He motioned for Luna to cross. She just clung onto a vine of ivy. She took a deep breath and jumped for dear life and landed in Louis' arms.

Then Rory sprinted across the sandy substance. Skill runs through that family. She too, jumped over vines of ivy, dodged breaths of fire, and then she held one wolves' paw. She then front flipped and landed, on her feet, on the platform. Wiping herself down.

Alexander flew across, carrying Rory's bag by his clutches.

Then Coco just ran for it. A piece of ivy wrapped around a strand of her hair, but she tugged it off, and then bounced onto the platform proudly.

Royal jumped and skipped across like it was some fun obstacle course, he just shoved his bag onto the platform and climbed onto it.

"I can't do this!" Beatrice yelled across the sand.

"You can! Just grab that piece of ivy right next to the bar. Cling to it and let it swing you across! Then jump!" Louis advised.

Beatrice put her red bag on her shoulder, and jumped onto the ivy vine. She squealed at first. Then she jumped, closing her eyes. She stumbled over onto her stomach when she landed but she made it across safely.

"Climb up, and, and we should be in the headquarters." Royal instructed.

Louis jumped up and climbed bravely. Then Coco climbed nervously, then Rory. Afterwards, Luna took a deep breath and climbed up. She wasn't entirely sure who was beneath her. But once all six of them had reached the wooden deck at the top. She touched the door handle.

Everyone nodded as she looked round for silent approval.

She pushed the door open. It creaked deafeningly, although Luna, and most likely everyone else, wanted those creaks to go on forever.

There were two tattooed men in vests playing poker and drinking whisky sitting at a table. There was a tall woman putting on red lipstick even though she already had a heavily applied layer on. There was an old man wrapping a bandage around the criminal's ankle, (where Luna had shot him the night at the manor), and Barney was sitting on a chair with a cigarette in his mouth. There was a muscled man raiding the cupboard with boxes of beer cans, some empty, at his feet. There was a group of around eight coal men attacking a small man with a doctor's cloak and glasses. There were three Devils feasting on a dead woman, and there was an abnormally vast wolf with violet eyes being petted by a woman wearing a black dress and holding a glass of wine in her free hand.

The floor was just as filthy as the vents. There were empty glasses scattered all over the place, and a rat was eating what looked like a lip.

"Ugh not you again." Barney said roughly, turning round and 'accidentally' kicking the old man in the head.

"Yes, us again. Problem?" Louis hissed.

"Actually yes. Our Devils are full. They couldn't eat you when you fail to defeat us."

Luna yelled, "Hmm. Well, if they're full then I suppose they can't finish off that poor woman, can they? Who even is it?"

"Some pathetic teenager named Rachel. Came in here to warn me that I was going to get thwarted!"

Coco jumped.

"Rachel?" Coco whispered. She peeked round the Devil and saw a flash of orange hair.

Louis pulled her back quickly as she started running to the Devil.

"Ha! You're just as idiotic as her!" Barney sneered.

"Where's your gun?" Luna asked, trying to act mean.

"Hmm. Well, I don't have it. I only have a Comporatora wolf, Coalins, and Devils." Barney chuckled.

"I believe my wife can explain what we're going to do to you if you, let's say, don't give us what we want." Barney giggled.

"Your wife? Oh my! That poor thing. Is she blind? You looked fifty times better when you were possessing that poor old guy. Now look at you." Coco replied.

The woman in the black dress downed her wine. "Actually, I think he looks more handsome than poor old Finley Hartio. And yes, if you don't give us, let's say, Copper, then, I'm afraid we will have no choice but to feed you to our lovely dog Halo." She had walked right up to Luna, her breath smelt of alcohol and mint.

"Luna, here." Rory whispered, passing her ribbon into Luna's hand behind her back. Luna gave her a thumbs up.

"Fine. Have me." Said Luna, walking happily up to Barney.

"Aww. Kids can be so thick." The woman said.

"Yes. We can be quite thick, but you're *certainly* not thin. Here! Let me help." Luna said. She hurriedly pulled the ribbon around his neck, and into a loose knot.

"Ha ha. Quick little rat you are."

"If I just pull this ribbon, you'll strangle until we call the police." Luna said happily. Grinning at the criminal.

"You wouldn't dare do that to your own uncle."

"Try me." Luna raised an eyebrow.

"Go on then. Strangle me. But I have many allies who would happily cut each and every one of your heads, off." Barney giggled.

"You've orphaned many children. You've killed millions. So now, it's time that poor Barney Nicho Bubwul got a taste of his own medicine." Luna pulled the ribbon. "Now." She said. The other five ran towards different people. Louis began fighting the Devils. Coco attacked Halo. Rory took the two women, Royal tried the coal men, or as they were officially called, Coalins. Beatrice attacked the two poker players and the raider of the cupboard. And Luna picked up the dial phone and called the American emergency line.

"What's your emergency?"

"Hi, hi, umm, me and my friends here have got the entire Bubwul crew surrounded. It's just up Mount Davis. Your station isn't far is it?"

"No no. Well done. Hold on, one moment. What is your name?"

"Luna, Luna Copper."

"Right. Thank you, Luna. That's a lovely name. Latin. I'm Cathy. Help is on the way."

"Thank you so much Cathy." Luna hung up.

Louis had surprisingly knocked all of the Devils unconscious with nothing but a lip bleeding and a bite wound on his forehead.

Halo was whining on the floor, and Coco had a bleeding ear and nose.

Rory was kicking her leg high enough to knock out the last woman. Her eye was bleeding a tad because one of the women had stuck her nail in it, but they were both lying on the floor.

Barney was trying to breathe on the floor.

Royal was supporting the skinny doctor and they were attacking the final Coalin.

Beatrice had a vast scrape right down the side of her face, and the raider of the cupboard was mumbling under his breath, but the two poker players were sprawled on the floor, and the raider had bubbly beer pouring out of his mouth.

Everyone heard sirens.

The six of them grinned.

Suddenly, a giant pair of wings crashed through the wall, with five officers on top. They jumped down and swiftly handcuffed all seventeen criminals. They then called the 'Rare Creature Authority'. To treat Halo. A kind woman took the dog by a lead into a large cage so that they could transport it to safety.

Rory, Coco, Royal, Louis, and Beatrice all approached Luna. Each of them grinned.

"You lot look like you've been in the wars." Said the female officer with a badge saying: Tracie.

"Can we please have your parent or guardians' mobile numbers? And your schools?" She asked, her glorious ginger hair flowing.

"I go to Uniqae." Rory said proudly.

"We are all Winged Beauties. Except for Beatrice." Luna said.

"No, no, I'm Winged Beauties. I just sit by the back." Beatrice answered.

They all gave their parents mobile numbers to Tracie, Coco gave James's number. Tracie phoned all of them saying that it was safe for them to go back to school, and told them what had happened.

Rory said goodbye to everyone else, and the officers dropped her off at Uniqae.

"We just did that. WE ACTUALLY DID THAT!" Coco yelled.

Everyone cheered and they found themselves wrapped in a hug.

"We can drop you off as well, at Winged Beauties. We have an extra vehicle." Said a tall police officer.

Everyone thanked him and they hopped in the vehicle.

After a couple hours of telling the police officer about themselves. They thanked him once more and jumped off at the gates of the school, they opened welcomingly as usual. And they entered.

Everyone had arrived. The words had spread like butter, as they entered the North Hall, everyone went quiet, they stopped their conversations. It was a moment of silence.

Then Anna and Skye stood up and clapped. Then Rogererare smiled and clapped his hands. Everyone cheered. Then clapped.

"Here stand the pupils who saved the world!" Rogererare yelled. Everyone cheered loudly. Even Jasmine clapped once or twice.

"To celebrate our success, everyone, go and change into your favourite clothes! Let's have an unplanned disco!" Rogererare sounded strange excited.

CHAPTER EIGHTEEN: THE END OF ONE, THE BEGINNING, OF ANOTHER

Luna arrived, wearing a white hoodie and jeans. No one had dressed up all fancy, Coco was wearing a blue jumpsuit, and she had cleaned up her nose and ear so that she was not covered in blood.

Louis had a red shirt on and black trousers. His hair had lost the dead rat.

Anna and Skye were talking to Beatrice in matching purple dresses. Beatrice was wearing a green jumpsuit, decorated with Winglets.

Royal dressed in his white t-shirt and denim trousers but just wiped them down.

"Louis Lochsmith, Coco Wheezleberry, Luna Copper, Beatrice Natalia, Royal Richards, please come up here." Rogererare instructed.

They scurried up.

"How does it feel?" Rogererare asked.

"Crazy."

"Weird."

"AWESOME!"

"Crazy."

"Joyful."

"And even though we've, 'saved the world' I hope that this isn't it. I hope, a new chapter begins here. And I want, everyone, to be involved." Louis yelled. All five of them looked up, to see the most wonderful thing possible.

At the stairs, wearing a denim jacket, and a pink skirt, walking down with a grin, was River. Her nose was a bit burnt at the side but that didn't matter.

Royal, Louis, Coco, Luna, and Beatrice, jumped down off the platform, and sprinted to where she stood, they wrapped their arms around her and each other. Royal uncharacteristically, wailed in disbelief. It was as if a miracle had spun over them. An incredible miracle. A heart mending miracle.

"What's that I hear about a new chapter eh?" River said, grinning.

"This is where the chapter ends River."

"Oh." She replied, miserably.

"And a newer, and better one begins." Said Luna, Coco, Louis, Beatrice, and Royal in unison.

"To a new chapter!" Said Coco, raising her glass of sparkling water.

"To a new chapter!"

Their glasses touched, wishing, for another miracle to come.

©Emma Tolcher, E.T Books Around the Corner. 03/03/2021

Printed in Great Britain
by Amazon

58208502R00122